GIRL IN THE TOWER
by
Jane Corby

Author of "NURSE'S ALIBI" *and*
"NURSE LIZA HALE"

Verity Welles, a young New York secretary, had inherited a half-interest in an art gallery in the Berkshires. Her partner was a middle-aged man married to a young wife; and the gallery was housed in a huge stone mansion filled with frightening sounds. But Verity was about to dismiss her fears concerning these as baseless—until her co-heir was strangled to death and her own life was threatened.

Then perforce she became suspicious of all the members of the household, including the murdered man's wife, an art expert; his turbaned valet from the Far East; and his handsome male secretary.

A collage of art, adventure, romance and suspense.

GIRL IN THE TOWER

GIRL IN THE TOWER

by

JANE CORBY

ARCADIA HOUSE

12

Printed in the United States of America

GIRL IN THE TOWER

Chapter 1

The gala to celebrate the arrival of several new paintings representing important artists of the modern school
in Italy was in full swing at Sky Towers, in the Hall of
Fame Gallery recently established in an old, old mansion, a palatial landmark in an almost deserted section of
New England.

A young man, his sun-streaked brown head of un-
tamed hair topping by several inches the girl who stood
nearby, looked closely at the picture of the signature,
found none and turned to her.

"Looks like a Giorgio de Chirico, doesn't it?" he remarked.

"It is."

"You sound absolutely sure."

"I am."

"Well!" said the young man. "I take it you're an
expert."

"I'm half owner of this gallery. You see, I know it's

authentic because. . . ."

"You're not going to talk art!" The young man sounded alarmed. "All I know about art I got from that movie about Michelangelo."

"All *I* know about art I learned since coming here just a little while ago. I was going to tell you that I know this painting is authentic because the artist's signature is on the back where he often signed his paintings. His signature, *Gi. de Chirico*, with sweeping 'C's,' is as famous as his actual pictures!"

The young man looked at her curiously. "If you're really a newcomer to this business, how did you ever acquire a half-interest in a gallery like this?" he asked. "And if I may make a personal remark, at your early age?"

"I inherited it," said the girl. "But don't you think, before we go into my affairs—and perhaps yours—any further, we ought to introduce ourselves?"

"I beg your pardon; I should have told you who I am the minute I spoke to you. But I was intrigued. Tynan Reynolds is the name. Called Ty, of course. I'm in the neighborhood by accident. I was looking for a place to continue working on a book I started eons ago, and a tire blew out just outside the village below. While waiting in the inn down there, I decided it was so deadly quiet that I . . . that's the whole story, except that the owner of the inn gave me his card of invitation to this do of yours. . . ."

"Verity Welles here. Have you met my partner, Jasper Wetherby, and his wife? She's Lilli Freer; uses her own name so that her contacts in Europe won't be confused. She says she's well known in Europe as a go-between."

"A go-between?"

"She arranges contacts between artists and buyers. I don't understand how it's done, exactly. She married Jasper Wetherby on his last buying trip to Europe. She's coming over. . . . Lilli Freer, may I present Tynan Reynolds, a writer?"

"You certainly may!" Lilli Freer, thirtyish, held out her hand.

"A would-be writer," said Ty. "Miss Welles exaggerates."

The remark annoyed Verity. "Will you two excuse me? I must speak to Rudy Bremer."

"Mr. Wetherby's secretary," explained Lilli, as Verity moved toward a handsome young man, so fair-haired as to be almost white, so sun-tanned as to be almost bronze.

Ty Reynolds' eyebrows shot up involuntarily.

"He looks like a film star," he remarked. He noticed that the secretary had taken Verity's arm and was leading her toward a door that opened into what appeared to be a formal garden. He glanced at Lilli, who was noticing it too. It seemed like a good time to introduce a new subject.

"I was just admiring that de Chirico painting," he observed. "I suppose it's expensive. I wish I could buy it."

"Giorgio de Chirico's works do come high," Lilli agreed. "One sold recently for $40,000."

"If I ever get my book finished, and if the movies buy it for, say, a million dollars, I'll talk to you again about buying a Chirico." Ty grinned.

"Here's hoping," said Lilli, smiling in turn. "Meanwhile—" she waved toward open double doors leading into the house—"there's a buffet table well worth your attention. I'm not only a hostess; I'm a hungry one. Will you?" Ty took her arm, and they joined in the slow-moving line that was trying to decide between out-sized shrimp, roast beef girdled with mushrooms, lobster, ham rolled delectably around wedges of cheese, avocado filled with only the chef knew what and a dozen varieties of sandwiches, to say nothing of such dazzling desserts as green grape tarts, strawberry mousse, many-tiered cakes and jello in fantastic shapes.

"Is your chef named Lucullus?" asked Ty, straight-faced.

"Sky Towers boasts nothing more impressive, in the culinary department, than a cook, name of Marietta, and a couple of village-girl helpers. All this was flown in. Ah, here we are!"

Lilli smiled at the waiter, who was holding a plate invitingly, and began to indicate her selections. They found a little table for two in a flower-garlanded recess, and Lilli chatted knowingly of European authors she had met and showed a charming interest in the book Ty was writing. Afterward she introduced Ty to some of the important guests.

But what, he asked himself, his gaze roving over the shifting crowd, had become of the girl with the lilac eyes, as he characterized Verity Welles mentally? Had that pale-haired giant abducted her? He edged his way gradually toward the garden door where he had seen them last, and made a nuisance of himself, peering over hedges at privacy-seeking couples. But Verity seemed to have vanished. He even thought of wandering around in the house, built around a hollow square, but looking up at its four surrounding walls, topped with turrets and festooned with balconies and hemming in the garden, he decided that any such expedition would meet with disapproval by the denizens of the place. He took a last look around and, seeing an ornate gate at one side, built into one of the house walls, went toward it and found it opened on a driveway with a footpath beside it. He took it without further hesitation and followed it down the mountainside to the village.

The party was over. Verity, in her remote third floor tower room, sat brushing her hair into a dark cloud around her shoulders. Rudy Bremer was the handsomest man she had ever met, she decided, meeting her own eyes, their odd lilac color now deepened, in the dimly lit room, to almost purple. They were eyes slightly tilted at the outer corners, under dilated black brows that matched her hair and emphasized the upward slant of the eyes themselves.

Rudy Bremer's English was flawless but tinged with the faintest trace of an accent. Verity could not place it. It reminded her of Lilli Freer's. They might have come from the same European background, wherever that was. Lilli had never divulged any facts about herself, beyond a vague outline of the way she had met Jasper Wetherby in Italy, guided him to some good art buys, as he said, and after an apparently whirlwind courtship, married him before leaving Europe. As for Rudy Bremer, no one had ever explained him at all, except for saying he was a discovery of Lilli's, a young man who was the perfect secretary, with his knowledge of art and commercial training, for the owner of a distinguished art gallery.

Verity tied back her hair with a ribbon and went to sit on the old yellowed wicker settee which was one of the room's charms for her. She wanted to look around and enjoy her nest high in the tower. The settee had cushions in pale yellow and deep gold, repeating the colors in the round rug on the floor, patterned in nasturtiums. The rug, Verity was sure, had been specially woven for the room, it was proportioned so carefully.

There were two of these towers, one at either of the front corners of the house, separated from each other by long corridors. The towers were built of solid masonry up to the second floor, where, as on the third floor, they had ornate doors opening into single rooms.

The house was a labyrinth of rooms, placed at odd angles and at different levels. It fascinated Verity and frightened her a little, all those vast echoing corridors and unexpected stairways. Why, she wondered, with the builder's evident fondness of stairways, was there no special stairway inside her tower? To reach her room she had to use one of the "public" staircases, from the second to the third floor, then enter through the tower door leading off the corridor.

"I wish I had a staircase all to myself, enclosed within the tower," she sighed now. "It would be so romantic!"

Lilli Freer had protested Verity's choice of a room

when she arrived at Sky Towers from New York.

"It's above the forecourt where the garage is located. There'll be traffic noises."

"I'm used to traffic noises. I'm from New York—remember?" said Verity. "I love nasturtium colors, and I particularly like the view—a glimpse of the lake and all those mountains marching north."

"But the ivy that has almost covered the windows doesn't permit much of a view," Lilli pointed out. "Now the other tower has a wonderful view, too, and no ivy to speak of. . . ."

Jasper Wetherby looked up irritably from the book he was reading.

"If the girl likes that tower room, let her have it. Squabbling over rooms in the house that has forty rooms!"

"Oh, you old bear!" Lilli crossed the library, where the three of them had gathered to await the dinner gong, and sat on the arm of Jasper's chair, ruffling his thick, curly white hair and then laying her cheek against it. "You know there aren't forty rooms in this house!"

"Thirty-nine then," said Jasper, laughing and reaching up to pat Lilli's bare shoulder.

He's nearly fifty and absolutely silly about her, thought Verity. I suppose, having been a bachelor for most of his life. . . . She didn't finish the thought, but said, after a moment:

"Thank you, Mr. Wetherby." The dinner gong sounded.

For the first time since coming to Sky Towers, Verity found it difficult to go to sleep the night after the party. There was a wind; it rattled the ivy at the windows. There were six of them—narrow slits, as befitted a tower —and as Lilli had pointed out at the beginning, they were half overgrown with green creepers. The ivy could be cut back a little, Verity decided. Not from all the windows— she liked the greenish underwater kind of light that filtered through by day. Why, she wondered for the hundredth time, had Lilli objected to her taking this room? Would she never get asleep?

She must have fallen asleep at last, for when she was awakened by a noise—and she wasn't quite sure that she had actually heard anything—she saw by her bedside clock it was two-thirty A.M. She sat up. Yes, there was a sound, a kind of soft sliding overhead. Footsteps, too. Very cautious footsteps that she could scarcely hear.

But Lilli had said there was nothing but a long-deserted attic overhead! Verity held her breath. The sounds ceased. Was it the wind, after all? She was sliding down again, reaching to pull up the yellow satin comforter—it got chilly up here on the mountain top in these eerie hours—when she heard the sound of a car starting up in the court below.

Verity listened intently. No, it was not going toward the garage. It was not a late-returning member of the household—or one of the household staff. The car was moving stealthily across the courtyard. After a moment she heard the distant faint clang of the forecourt gates. Someone was taking the trouble to shut them after the car went through. She heard nothing but the wind after that. The car could coast soundlessly down the long, ,winding driveway.

Verity crept to her door, opened it a crack and listened. Perhaps someone had been taken ill, and it was the doctor's car she had heard. But it sounded heavy, like a truck, she thought. Besides, that wouldn't account for the sounds she had heard above her room. The house was silent. There was no sound of a carefully closing door.

Verity was suddenly frightened. The house was so still. And, she realized, she was alone in the tower; alone, in fact, in that end of the house. The rooms that opened off the corridor on the third floor were, as far as she knew, unoccupied. Jasper Wetherby and his Lilli had an enormouse double suite on the second floor. Rudy Bremer had a bedroom and bath, also on the second floor, but around the corner, past the door of that second tower and off the corridor that formed the side of the square. Aunt Margaret, who had accompanied Verity from New York, had a pleasant two-room suite on the ground floor. She demurred at stairs, and the old-fashioned elevator, which nobody used anyway, looked dangerous to her.

Verity was trembling when she shot the bolt on her door— the first time since she had been at Sky Towers— and threw herself into bed.

I might as well be alone in this house, she thought, shuddering. I could move. . . .

Next morning she felt differently, however. There must be a reasonable explanation of the sounds she had heard. She would investigate and settle the question in her own mind. After all, she was half owner of the place; she had a right to know what, if anything, was going on in the top of the tower.

The opportunity came on a day when Jasper Wetherby had gone off to act as guest speaker for an exhibit in a nearby town and had taken Rudy Bremer with him. Lilli Freed was in the village, having her car repaired. This was the time to investigate the attic.

A short stairway from the third floor led to the half-story attic of the house. But there was no entrance on this floor to the tower attic. Could it open on the roof?

An iron ladder, allmost straight up and down, with a trap door at the top, probably led to the roof. She tried the trap door; it was heavy, but she managed to pry it up. Sure enough, she found herself on the roof, on a kind of promenade, protected by a low parapet. There it was—a low door in the tower wall.

This door, however, was locked. She'd have to ask Mrs. Mullins, the housekeeper, for the key. Turning, she was making her way along the walk when she saw Lilli, just emerging from the trap door.

"*What* are you doing?" cried Lilli.

"Just looking around." Verity tried to sound casual.

Lilli stepped forward, a queer light in her eyes. She raised her hand as if to seize the girl. It flashed through Verity's mind that she meant to push her over the parapet.

Chapter 2

When Lilli's hand descended, it was only to pat Verity's shoulder. The girl just managed to smother a gasp.

"If I were you, I wouldn't wander around this ancient castle by myself," said Lilli. "The place hasn't yet been completely restored, you know. There are floors that might give way, ceilings that have already fallen.

"Anyway, you know what killed the cat. . . ." She smiled and motioned for Verity to precede her on the way down.

Later, taking a walk to the village, Verity descended the long, curving drive and took herself to task for being so easily frightened, as she had been on the roof. It was just the strangeness of her surroundings, she felt.

In the village, Verity leaned on the wooden railing of the little bridge that spanned a creek which ran right through the middle of town. Looking down at the tumbling brown-gold water, breaking into frills of white foam where it encountered high stones, she set determinedly to straighten out her thinking.

She considered Aunt Margaret's view. Sky Towers, that somewhat apprehensive lady had said when Verity first broached the idea of going there, was a dangerous place for a young girl alone in the world.

"I'm twenty-two," Verity had countered. "And I've been earning my way as a secretary for eighteen months! Why shouldn't I go to Sky Towers, since I'm a half-owner?"

"You never even met this partner of your late uncle, for one thing. You know nothing about art, for another. If you want my advice, I'd suggest you sell your share of the business and use the money to take a cruise some place. You might meet some eligible young men, which you'll never do in that wild mountain country."

Verity had laughed. "There's nothing wild about a New England mountain. No Indians lurking behind the murmuring pines and hemlocks, looking for girls to scalp. But if you don't want to come with me, Aunt Margaret. . . ."

"I'm your own father's sister. I've brought you up since you were ten years old and left an orphan after your father and mother were killed in that terrible car crash, and if you think I'm going to turn you out into the world. . . ."

Verity smiled down into the water, remembering. Now

that she was ensconced at Sky Towers, Aunt Margaret seemed happy enough, although critical of Lilli Freer—who knows what kind of life she really had in Europe?—and "scared to death," in her own words, of "that fellow in the turban." Yet she had settled down comfortably in her first floor suite, two rooms and bath.

One thing she had in common with Lilli Freer: she disapproved of Verity's choice of the tower room.

"But you could be near me," suggested Verity. "There are any number of unused rooms on the third floor, close to my tower."

"The stairs would kill me," said Aunt Margaret. "And don't tell me there's the elevator. That old-fashioned piece of junk—I wouldn't trust myself in it if the house were on fire!"

Aunt Margaret's suite included a kitchenette, built into one corner of her sitting room, where she could prepare snacks for herself when she did not feel like joining the others at meals. At times she preferred her own cooking to that of Marietta, the cook. She carried on guerrilla warfare with Mrs. Mullins, the housekeeper, liked the butler, who was obsequious and hardly ever said anything to her but "Yes, Madam," thought the three housemaids impertinent, gave the gardener and his helpers the benefit of her advice on horticulture and regarded the chauffeur and the couple in the gatehouse as outlanders, not worth her attention.

About Rudy Bremer, Jasper Wetherby's secretary, Aunt Margaret reserved her opinion. But:

"I think he's attracted to you," she told Verity. "With those beautiful continental manners of his, I rather think he must come of a very good family. He might even be a nobleman, who because of those wars and all, has become impoverished and therefore took this job as Mr. Wetherby's secretary. Now, if he should manage to re-establish his claim to a family fortune and large estates. . . ."

"Even without a fortune he's attractive." Verity laughed. "But what I'm here for, Aunt Margaret, is to take my uncle's place as Mr. Wetherby's partner and help promote the art gallery."

Verity did not share her aunt's distrust of the inhabitants of Sky Towers, not even of Lilli Freer. She had been wary of Lilli at first, but the older woman had been going out of her way to make Verity happy, the girl realized. "That fellow in the turban," to whom Aunt Margaret referred, was Omar, a valet-man-about-the-house Jasper had brought home with him from the Far East, who only required getting used to. Except for his turban and odd slippers, with long, turned up toes, he wore commonplace American clothes.

There had been really nothing in her welcome to

Sky Towers to make her uneasy, Verity decided now, as she turned her back on the creek and started toward the great iron gates that guarded the entrance to the driveway. They were standing open, as they often did, at Lilli Freer's orders.

"We don't want the village people to think we're upstaging them," she had explained, and Jasper Wetherby, inclined as he was to agree with most of her edicts, smiled his assent to this. Verity had been present during this interchange, and Mrs. Mullins, who happened to be standing by for orders, also, like Verity, smiled approval. Mrs. Mullins was a village product herself, and so were the three housemaids.

Now, walking slowly up the rising, twisting driveway, Verity caught her breath as, rounding a turn, she was confronted with a ten-foot hedge of mountain laurel in full bloom. The varying shades of pink, deep, luscious pink where the sun sought out the blossoms, nearly pure white where the sun failed to penetrate between the great boughs of thick, glossy leaves, brought Verity to a standstill.

She broke off a small spray and walked on. The sight of so much sheer beauty had quashed the uneasiness she had felt since encountering Lilli on the rooftop. Sky Towers was a beautiful place. When she got used to it and understood better the people there, she would be able to laugh at her easily roused suspicions.

"Verity, is that you?"

Verity, passing Jasper's study door, turned and looked in as she returned from her walk.

"You've met Mr. Reynolds, haven't you? He told me he was here at our recent open house. Stop a minute, will you, Vee?"

Ty Reynolds stood up as the girl came in.

"The house fascinated me, the glimpse I had of it that day," he said. "It gave me an idea, and Mr. Wetherby has been good enough to listen and approve. I want to change the background of my book, using this house."

"Good publicity for the gallery," said Jasper. "The house has quite a history, I believe, and there are documents and records in the library here that are worth examination. Fellow who built it in the eighteenth century was an Englishman. Left England under a cloud—don't know what he'd done—but he belonged to an important family, living in a castle and throwing their weight around all over that part of the country. When our boy fled, it seems he had first lined his pockets, and he built this house as nearly a replica of the family shack as he could."

"How long ago was that?" asked Verity.

"Dates back to pre-Revolutionary times, I think. Your

Uncle Timothy, Vee, paid more attention to what the real estate fellows were talking about than I did. But I understand there's a hand-written diary in the library that the builder—slightly daft, if you ask me—left behind him. Why don't you and Mr. Reynolds look around and see what you can find?"

"Your Uncle Timothy—does he live here, too?" asked Ty, when they were unlocking the huge old desk where Jasper had told them the house records were kept.

"Uncle Timothy Welles and his wife, Aunt Eloise, were killed in a plane accident soon after buying this house. I'm the last surviving member of the Welles family, and Uncle Timothy left me his estate, including a partnership in the art gallery. There's a proviso that if I die unmarried, everything reverts to Jasper Wetherby."

"And when he dies, Lilli Freer gets the lot, naturally."

"Jasper has arranged for that, I understand. Lilli Freer wouldn't have any trouble running the business. Jasper says she has forgotten more about art than he will ever learn. Exaggerated, that statement, I suppose, but Lilli does seem to be an internationally recognized expert."

"Let's hope she won't be called upon to run the business," said Ty. "Try to prevent it, will you?"

"Oh, I'm planning to live to a ripe old age," Verity

assured him, lifting out of the desk's deepest drawer several flat leather volumes that looked promising.

"And since we're on the subject of your uncle's last will and testament, Vee, perhaps I may be permitted a personal query. Uncle Timothy's reference to marriage: are you, that is, are you . . .?"

"Neither married nor engaged, if that's what you're asking," laughed Verity. "And you . . .?"

"Ditto," said Ty. "Are you interested?"

Verity was saved from answering Ty's provocative question by the arrival of Lilli. They explained Ty's interest in the history of Sky Towers.

"Good!" said Lilli. "Things are slow around here today. Why not explore? I'll go with you. We'll collect Rudy Bremer, who's been over the route by himself, he told me, and can serve as a guide." He can point out danger spots, the years' toll of floors and ceilings."

"You'll need flashlights," Rudy Bremer told them when he was located. "The way the sky is darkening before a storm, we'll have to depend on them to examine some of the hideaway corners. The whole place hasn't been electrified, either."

Ty got only a token tour of the ground floor, since he had already seen the main rooms while the gala was in progress. Unexpected staircases led to a maze of corridors on the second floor, some of them opening into little turrets, too small to be used as rooms and serving, Lilli remarked, only to accumulate dust.

"They might have been meant as prisoners' cells," said Ty. "Some of them have iron rings built into the walls, probably to anchor chains to somebody's unlucky legs."

At the front of the house, they looked into the tower opposite the one which belonged, as she put it, to Verity. The room at the second floor level was a card room.

"Will you look at that chess set!" cried Rudy, opening an ornately carved box to reveal a handsome set of ivory and ebony chessmen. "I could use this. Anybody for chess?"

"It's a lovely chess set," said Verity wistfully. "I only wish I could play."

"I'll teach you," Rudy assured her. "Say when?"

"Tonight . . ." Verity began hesitatingly.

"Tonight," Ty interrupted, "she has promised to go dancing with me. Try again, Big Boy."

Rudy turned away without answering. "At the opposite end of this corridor, under Verity's room, is the gun collection."

He took Verity's arm, and the other two fell in step behind them, Ty humming a marching song under his breath. He was feeling elated at having turned aside Rudy's invitation so neatly, Verity thought, wondering

if the date to go dancing, of which she had not heard
before, really was a serious offer.

The gun room was impressive. It was Jasper Wetherby's own collection, which he had sent up from New
York at the time he transferred his personal possessions
to Sky Towers, along with the Hall of Fame Gallery.
Rudy Bremer, it was soon apparent, was an expert on
antique firearms and other lethal weapons. He glibly
described the origin and use of the objects displayed.

"Many of these weapons come from out-of-the-way
places," Rudy explained. "Mr. Wetherby picked them
up all over the world during his travels—he is an inveter-
ate traveler."

"That bit of belt, is it? That can't be a weapon!"
Verity was looking at an innocent-appearing cord fast-
ened in a prominent place to the wall.

"That's a thugee cord," said Rudy. "Mr. Wetherby's
very proud of it. He picked it up in India—rather rare
now, I believe."

"It looks harmless," said Verity.

"It's a very effective method of strangulation." Rudy
stared reflectively at the cord. "More than a century
ago it was the favorite weapon of a band of robbers and
assassins, called Thugs, in India. They worked in bands,
robbing and murdering travelers by using this type of
cord. It was neat, no blood involved, and was con-

nected with their religious practices."

"Horrible!" Lilli shuddered. "I'd prefer to use that cute short curved sword over there." She lifted it down from the wall as she spoke.

"That's a scimitar," Rudy said. "Used in the old days by the Turks and the people then called Persians. Be careful—it has a fine edge even now."

"I wonder how you use it," murmured Lilli, swishing it from side to side, then raising it above her head.

At that moment the storm broke. A blinding flash of lightning was followed by a roar of thunder that seemed to shake the solid tower. It was an instant before, with the thunder grumbling off in the distance and darkness succeeding the lightning flash which had lit up the whole landscape outside, the group in the gun room realized that it was totally dark inside, too.

The lights were out!

Verity screamed. It was a cry of pain.

"Oh! What have I done?" It was Lilli's voice.

Ty turned his flashlight on Verity, who was clutching her shoulder. Lilli stood beside her, the scimitar still in her hand.

"I was startled," she stammered. "I had the sword over my head—the lightning—the thunder—I let my arm fall . . ."

At that moment the lights came on again. Ty, slipping his flashlight into his pocket, was examining Verity's shoulder, pushing away the narrow strap of her sleeveless blouse.

"The skin is not broken," he said. "A glancing blow must have hit your shoulder. Luckily it was not the point of the blade. Does it hurt much?"

"It doesn't hurt at all—now." Verity smiled ruefully at the concerned faces around her. "I screamed from fright, I guess, and of course it hurt for just a second. Great soldier I'd make, wouldn't I?"

Nobody laughed.

"It could have been serious," said Rudy, taking the scimitar from Lilli's hand and replacing it on the wall.

"I feel so stupid," Lilli said in a small voice. "Why, I could have killed her!"

"I'm not so easily killed!" Verity touched Lilli's hand. "Don't feel badly about it. It was an accident."

"A lucky accident," said Rudy.

"Let's get out of here," suggested Ty. "I don't suppose a tower is the safest place in a storm, anyway. Even one that that has stood for—what did that diary say, Verity?"

"Two hundred years, give or take a decade," said Verity. She smiled. Not for the world would she let them know her shoulder did hurt.

Chapter 3

Verity chose a dress with a rather high neck, one that hid the black and blue mark which, as she expected, had shown up on her shoulder where the flat of the scimitar blade had struck. Ty had managed to get her aside after they had decided there'd been enough touring of the house, soon after her accident, and he invited her belatedly to the dancing date he had claimed before the others.

At first she had demurred.

"But you'll have to go," said Ty. "What kind of idiot will I look like if Lilli and the rest find out I hadn't even asked you before?"

"That, it seems to me, is your problem," retorted Verity.

"Yeah," admitted Ty. "There's a line I remember about *'La dame sans merci.'* I'm not sure of my French, but you get the idea. It describes you."

"Is the editing intentional? Because —"

"What do you mean, 'editing'?" demanded Ty.

"The line you're quoting goes, 'La belle dame,' " said Verity.

"Oh oh! When you're the most *'belle'* girl I ever saw—"

"Don't overdo it."

"But I couldn't possibly overdo my appreciation of you. You're a work of art. Aw, c'mon, Vee; let's have a fun evening."

Verity smiled. "What time?"

I went off to his room at the village inn to put on something "worthy of my first date with you," he told Verity, and she climbed to her tower to put on the flowered nylon she had bought before leaving New York. Dressed, and with a velvet bow in her hair, she went downstairs and was observing the effect in the ceiling-to-floor mirror in the front drawing room—there were three such formal rooms—when Lilli came in.

"Very pretty, Vee darling," said Lilli. "Have a good time. I'll wait up for you."

"But there's no need of that!" Verity spun around to stare in astonishment at the older woman. "I can take care of myself. I've had dates before, in New York, at that."

"The circumstances weren't quite the same, were they? Probably they were with men you knew well, and after all, what do we know about Tynan Reynolds?"

"Why, he's a writer."

"He says. But I've never seen his name in any list of current authors."

"Of course not! He's just starting. He's working on his first book."

"And meanwhile, I suppose he'd find it useful to have a rich wife to support him."

"Lilli dear, you're talking nonsense. I'm going out dining and dancing, not to get married!" Verity laughed. "Besides, I'm not rich."

"You will be some day—you've got prospects. All this—" she waved her arm in a sweeping gesture to indicate Sky Towers—"the gallery—"

They both heard the sound of a motor outside and the door chimes a second after.

"Ty's here," murmured Verity, moving to the door.

Lilli followed her, put an arm around her and kissed her cheek. "Be on your guard," she whispered.

"Don't worry about me," Verity said in a low voice. "But it's good of you to take an interest."

The butler had opened the door to Ty, but Verity ran out into the hall to meet him. She didn't want Lilli to give Ty any admonitions. Lilli was only solicitous, she was thinking, but she needn't take a mother-hen attitude toward her. She was barely thirty herself, Verity knew. Just because she happened to be married to an older man, there was no reason for her to assume guardianship over her, Verity was thinking as Ty took her hand. They ran down the steps to the car, laughing like two children.

The afternoon storm had washed the air clean and left the road glistening in this remote area, where cars were infrequent after dark. Their lights silvered the still dripping branches on either side, and the heavy scent of pine reminded them that there were forest remnants all around them.

"Here stands the forest primeval," began Verity.

"Mostly second or third growth now," said Ty. "The denizens of the wild have long since departed, I expect."

"I suppose," said Verity, her head against the back of the seat. "You'll never convince Aunt Margaret, though, that no danger lurks within and without Sky Towers, but especially within."

"She may not be so far wrong at that," said Ty. "That's an odd assortment of people you've got there."

Verity sat up straight. "What makes you say that? Uncle Timothy once told Aunt Margaret that Jasper

Wetherby was 'the salt of the earth'. And the others—
they're there because he wants them there. What can you
possibly mean?"

"You've heard of the art scandal in Europe?"

"No. Is there one? And what has that to do with
Jasper Wetherby and Lilli and the rest?"

"Nothing perhaps. But it's too complicated to explain while I'm steering this car up hill and down dale.
It never occurred to the mountain road builders to by-
pass a few curves, did it? Wait till we get to the Tyrol
Arms, which is where we're going, by the way. Back
at my little inn, they say it's got good food and disco
dancing."

Verity didn't answer. She was disturbed by Ty's words,
and reminded vividly of her sense of uneasiness, which
she had tried to repress, ever since coming to Sky
Towers. Also, she was remembering the unexplained
sounds overhead in her own tower room, and the way
Lilli had tried to discourage her from investigating the
tower attic. But Lilli had been only taking care of her,
she had since decided.

The Tyrol Arms was as attractive as Ty had heard.
It was a small place, and tonight there were just enough
customers to give it an air of festivity. They ate dinner
at a table for two, sitting on wooden chairs, painted
bright green, with seat cushions covered with flowered

cotton and a matching flowered tablecloth.

In the middle of the table was a fat candle in a sturdy wooden candle-holder, augmenting the romantically dim lighting from shaded wall lamps. They had soup in long-handled earthen bowls and ate Swiss-cheese soufflé in pastry shells and warm Tyrolean fruit cake.

"What about this art scandal of yours?" asked Verity, when they were waiting for the dessert to be served. "Is it serious?"

"Serious enough to warrant a high-powered investigation," said Ty. "I doubt if Jasper Weatherby is involved in it; still—"

"You'll never make me believe my Uncle Timothy was involved in anything shady." Verity's voice was firm. "I'd as soon suspect his sister, Aunt Margaret, of skulduggery. And if you knew her, you'd realize just how unlikely such a thing would be."

"Of course, honest people can be dupes," Ty pointed out, "especially when so much money is at stake, as in this case, and the crooks are at great pains to cover their tracks."

The dessert came, and they both gave it their full attention for a few minutes.

"Money seems so important to so many people," Verity sighed after a few minutes.

"I think of it now and then," said Ty dryly. "It can be useful, you know."

"Women often marry for money," pursued Verity, mindful of Lilli's hint about Ty's looking for a rich wife. "Men seem to put other things first."

"Oh, I don't know," Ty said teasingly. "It all depends. A talented fellow might find a rich wife just what he needs to permit him to develop his special gifts, unhampered by having to make a living."

Verity realized he was teasing her, but—the idea wasn't new to him! She finished her dessert thoughtfully.

They dropped all serious discussion to dance for a while, but Verity turned sober again when they were sitting on the terrace, watching the moon above the pointed tops of the tall evergreens.

"Tell me about this trouble in Europe," she urged. "I am a co-owner of an art gallery, you know. I ought to know what's going on commercially, even if I don't know anything about art."

"It's in the field of modern Italian art," said Ty.

"Just what we specialize in," breathed Verity.

"A fake art ring is suspected of copying the work of well-known artists, then extorting huge sums from tourists who are buying mostly to impress the folks at home. There's a possibility that much of this fake art is being unloaded on American galleries."

"That's dreadful," said Verity, frowning. "But I thought there were experts who vouched for the authenticity of works of art."

"There are certain experts who are under suspicion, too."

"I don't believe Jasper Wetherby can be fooled. And there's Lilli, who knows as much about Italian art as anyone in Europe, I've often heard him say."

"Possibly true. Still, if Jasper and Lilli—I'm only warning you to keep your eyes and ears open, and if you see or hear something that rouses your suspicions, maybe you'll report to me. I don't know what I could do, but—"

"But what?" demanded Verity, when Ty paused.

"I don't want to frighten you, but if Wetherby happens to have any connections with the European ring—you know so little about art, though, that I suppose you're safe."

"Safe from what?"

"You're a kind of intruder, Vee. You must see that. They can't prevent you from living here, under the terms of your uncle's will, and there's always the danger that if they are involved in something illegal, you'll accidentally discover it.

"Another thing, if anything happened to remove you from the scene—"

"Like being killed, you mean?"

"I don't mean anything, really. But Sky Towers has its dangers, I want to emphasize."

"I suppose you're thinking of the part of Uncle Timothy's will that says Jasper will inherit my share of the gallery if I die before I'm married. You know what, Ty Reynolds? I think you worry too much. Either that, or you're trying to scare me. But I don't see why you'd want to do that." Vee stood up. "Let's dance. I'm going to forget everything you've said."

"I hope you don't mean that."

Ty did not refer to the art scandal again, and they danced as light-heartedly as if there had been no disquieting discussion, but Verity could not quite keep Ty's insinuations from thrusting themselves into her mind. More than once she almost told Ty of the un-accounted—for noises in the attic above her room. Something stealthy had been going on, she was sure of that. But Lilli had warned her against Ty, and she trusted Lilli.

On the drive home, Ty talked of his book, and was enthusiastic about the material he had found for it in the library at Sky Towers.

"Those old diaries and notes are just what I need. I don't suppose Mr. Wetherby will allow me to carry away the originals, and hand-written copies are too time-consuming. Now, if I knew someone who would take down on the typewriter the parts I would like to use verbatim—"He glanced sideways at Verity.

"If you want to read them to me, I'll take them down," she said carelessly. "I don't have too much to do here. Or maybe Rudy Bremer would—"

"Rudy Bremer!"

"You sound horrified," laughed Verity.

"I am. I can't stand the sight of the guy. His poses, his pretensions—"

"You're being unjust. Rudy can't very well help looking like a Greek god in bronze, and his knowledge of art is not pretense. At least Lilli says it's not."

"There's something about him—I'm sure he's a phoney."

"My goodness, Ty, isn't there anybody at Sky Towers you approve of?"

"There is. A girl with midnight hair and lilac eyes."

"That's a spur-of-the-moment approval. Wait till you know her better." Verity grinned up at him mischievously.

"You wouldn't have dared say that if we weren't right at the front door of Sky Towers. The open front door, too, and Lilli Freer is in it."

It was true. Lilli was standing in the wide open doorway, with the lighted hall outlining her slim figure and gilding her otherwise nondescript hair. Verity stared at her in frustration. She had been sure Ty was about to kiss her, and now—

"Lilli! I told you not to wait up!" Verity opened the door of the car and jumped out without waiting for Ty to assist her.

"Coming in, Ty?" she asked.

"Yes," said Lilli, before Ty could answer. "It's very late, but come in if you like."

"Thank you, but no," said Ty. "Good night, everybody!" He started the car with a jerk without waiting for a reply, turned it amid flying gravel and whirled off down the gravel.

"You hurt his feelings." Verity followed Lilli into the house and stood by while she locked and bolted the door.

"Hurt his feelings! I don't see why. I invited him in."

It was hard to figure Lilli out, Verity was thinking as she went toward the stairs. She caught a glimpse of a light from Aunt Margaret's room down the corridor as she put her foot on the first step. She sighed.

I couldn't be better protected if I had the Secret Service watching me, she told herself, irritated. Nevertheless she went on down the hall to bid Aunt Margaret good night, and convince her that she had been returned in good order.

It was after she had left Aunt Margaret's rooms, and was on her way upstairs, that she looked down over the banister in time to see the shadowy figure of Omar disappearing through the far door of the long front drawing room. His white turban stood out in the dimness, the faint light provided by the one bracket still lit in the hall.

Now what's he up to? Verity had half a mind to pursue him and demand an explanation of this surveillance. But the other half of her mind was frightened. She ran upstairs and was breathless as she closed and locked her tower door behind her.

Chapter 4

The days passed, three of them. Ty Reynolds did not appear at Sky Towers. He did not even call her on the phone, and Verity wondered about it, as she reported to Jasper Wetherby every morning, at his request, to handle some of the office work. This was Rudy Bremer's job, but Jasper explained that Rudy was busy with some special work in his studio.

The studio, on the first floor next to Aunt Margaret's suite, was always locked, Verity had noticed. He liked to work without being interrupted, Lilli had explained. He was a "temperamental" painter, "a genius," and could not bear to have observers "looking over his shoulder" when he was in one of his artistic moods.

Verity was not surprised to learn that Rudy was a painter. Like Lilli, he could talk with authority on art in general and modern art in particular. From vague references he made to his life in Europe, she gathered that he had studied with famous artists and had even remarked, laughingly, that he could imitate the brushwork of this or that artist, so that the artist himself could not tell the difference.

Lilli frowned, overhearing this boast. "Don't say such stupid things, Rudy," she said sharply. "If Verity should repeat that in front of people who know something about art, she'd be laughed at."

Verity, who happened to be looking at Rudy's face, caught a strange expression in his eyes. It was as if he were about to make a spirited retort to Lilli, but refrained, with a great effort.

Verity was thinking of this incident as she filed away the last of the papers Jasper had given her and made her way along the twisting corridor that led to Aunt Margaret's room. She had a present for her—a little carved figure of a wildcat. An old man in the village carved these figures out of wood, none too recognizably, but Verity always stopped to buy one when she passed his cottage.

"Hi, Aunt Margaret! Something for you!" she cried, knocking lightly on her aunt's door and opening it at the same time. "Why, where are you?"

She glanced around the empty sitting room and was about to cross to the bedroom when Aunt Margaret's head appeared around the open panel of one side of the kitchenette. This utilitarian recess was usually closed off at this time of day. Verity's aunt had a finger to her lips, and she was beckoning to her niece with the air of a conspirator. Verity tiptoed to the recess as Aunt Margaret turned her back and moved close to the inner wall.

"Botheration!" she cried. "He's pushed something against it!" She came out into the sitting room, carefully closing the panels behind her. "I did want you to see what you'd make of it."

"Of what?" demanded Verity.

"There's a peephole in the wall back there. Isn't it thrilling? Just like in a real castle, where there were always intrigues going on and spies everywhere. I could see almost the whole room, by moving my head a little."

"But isn't that Rudy Bremer's studio next door?"

"Aunt Margaret!" Verity's voice sounded shocked. "You don't mean to tell me you've been spying on Rudy!"

"I only just now discovered the peephole," said Aunt Margaret in an aggrieved tone. "If I'd known about it sooner—"

"Rudy Bremer keeps his studio locked because he doesn't want people to watch him paint. I told you about that."

"That's all right," said Aunt Margaret comfortably. "He wasn't painting just now. That's why I wanted you to get a look; you'd probably figure out what he was doing to that painting. Wait, I tell you—"

"I don't want to hear!"

"High and mighty, aren't you? And to me, of all people! I'll tell you anyway. He was taking a picture out of a frame."

Verity gave a sigh of relief. "Nothing strange about that, was there? He sometimes has to make repairs of one kind or another on frames that get damaged in shipment. Pictures that are shipped from small European towns are often carelessly boxed. . . ."

"But you haven't heard all of it. As he lifted out the picture, I saw that there was another picture behind it!"

"Oh, Aunt Margaret! How do you know what you were looking at? You couldn't have had much of a view from that tiny little peephole."

"My goodness gracious! If I didn't forget to close the place up! It was really plugged up, but I saw that the plug was loose, and I dug it out with a nail file. . . ." She dashed back to the kitchenette and emerged again in a moment.

"I wouldn't want Rudy looking through from *his* side." She chuckled.

Verity laughed too. "Seriously, Aunt Margaret, I wouldn't for the world have Rudy think we're spying on him. He's so straightforward himself. . . ."

"Good-looking into the bargain! I could fall for him myself, if I were twenty years younger. I don't blame you, sweetie. Well, we'll settle this once and for all. You go find some glue, and we'll fix that plug so fast into the wall that it can never be pried loose again."

Verity went off to get the glue. When she returned, she reported that she had seen Rudy go into the art gallery, so they could work at the wall without as Margaret said, having him think that an army of mice was being mobilized for an invasion of his studio.

Aunt Margaret liked the carved wildcat so much that she decided she wanted to wear it for a pin, and Verity promised to have it fixed at once.

Later, in the afternoon, Verity was sitting beside an umbrella table on the terrace. It had been a hot day, and she was hoping for a stray breeze as the sun began to slide toward the west. Omar brought her a tall glass of lemonade without her asking for it. She thanked him, and he bowed. He spoke English so badly that he seldom spoke at all when he could avoid it, except to Jasper Wetherby, who knew something of the valet's native tongue and could follow his strange mishmash of the English language. Omar, turning away and looking back at the smiling Verity at the same time, nearly collided with Rudy Bremer, coming swiftly across the terrace.

"You clumsy idiot!" Rudy gave him a violent shove. Omar kept his balance with difficulty.

"The poor fellow was looking back at me to see if I wanted something to go with the lemonade he just brought," Verity said quickly.

"I can't stand him—reminds me of a slithering snake." Rudy set down the paraphernalia with which he was loaded. "I've been looking all over for you, darling. How about a game of chess?"

As he spoke, he unfolded the legs of the small table he had been carrying and began to take the chessmen out of the box.

"Why, that's the lovely set we saw in the game room!" exclaimed Verity. "I shouldn't be playing with that, when I don't know one figure from the other."

"You know the king from the queen," said Rudy, holding up the figures as he spoke. "And here's a knight and this castle, just like the one you live in."

He explained the basic rules of the game, while Verity listened attentively. She sighed.

"I'll never be like those chess fans who spend hours staring at the chessmen without making a move."

"Oh, professionals!" Rudy dismissed such earnest players with a shrug. "You'll manage, after a few more lessons. You have a quick intelligence in that charming head."

"I'm not trying to be more stpuid than I have to be." Verity laughed. She finished her lemonade, which she had neglected in her concentration on Rudy's explanations.

After a while, having mutually agreed that they had had enough chess for the day, Rudy folded up the table, placed the chessmen carefully in their box and carried everything to the side of the terrace door into the house.

"I'll get Omar to take it back to the game room. Give him something to do besides hang around mooning at you."

"Rudy!"

"On second thought, maybe I better not. He might drop the box and break something—or steal it."

"Stop it, Rudy! You know you don't believe a word of what you're saying."

"Don't I, though! You're a trusting child, aren't you? Mind if I sit down here?" He had pulled a lounge chair close to where Verity was sitting and waited for her nod before settling himself in it. That was one of the things she liked about Rudy Bremer, Verity was thinking: his way of deferring to her wishes.

They were companionably silent for a while, looking at the rolling mountains and the changing patterns of the shadows made by the lazily floating clouds.

"Must be some good climbing around here," observed

Rudy. "Are you a good climber?"

"I wouldn't know," said Verity. "I've never tried to climb a mountain."

"You have so much to learn," smiled Rudy. "I'll have to teach you—if you'll let me."

"I suppose you've climbed the Alps and mountains everywhere."

"I've done a bit of climbing. I even spent one vacation in the Himalayas."

"I've heard of them," said Verity politely.

"I should think you had. The highest range in the world."

"And when you climbed them, what did you see? The other side of the mountain?" Verity was flippant.

"I didn't explore any unclimbed peaks, but I saw some wonderful sights. Walls of sheer ice, great stretches of woods, bamboo, rhododendron—"

"Just like this part of the good old U.S.A.," said Verity. "The rhododendron, I mean. It grows around here."

"And such a lot of different birds," Rudy went on. "And just looking up at some of the peaks is something never to be forgotten. They look as if they were sheathed in silver. But the actual climbing isn't all joy. There's terrific heat to be endured, and the glare of the sun on snow, the difficulty of breathing in the rarefied air—oh, various discomforts at different levels. But it's an experience."

"I think I'd like to try some mountain climbing. Not in the Himalayas, of course, but around here in the Berkshires. History has been made in some of these mountains. Did you know that our mountains are millions of years older than the Rockies?"

"Did you know," Rudy returned, "that you look about twelve years old right now?"

Verity flushed. "You mean I look retarded?"

"You know very well I meant nothing of the sort. I've a good mind—" He broke off abruptly as Lilli appeared in the doorway.

"Don't let me stop you, Rudy. You've a good mind to do what?"

"You probably won't believe this," he said imperturbably, "but I was going to say I've a good mind to call Lilli and ask her to give Verity here some facts about chess and its history."

"You're right: I don't believe it." Lilli grinned amiably at Rudy. "But I'm perfectly willing to give a lecture on the origin of chess. By the way, have you told Verity that I'm a better chess player than you are, and that if you'd wanted a partner, I've been available most of the afternoon?"

"I wasn't looking for a partner, my pet. I was teach-

ing Verity here how to play, so that she can be my partner on afternoons when you're *not* available."

They exchanged long glances, which Verity could
not interpret. It was almost as if they were speaking to
each other without words. Verity had noticed such looks
before and wondered a little about it. Still, both being in
the art field—Besides, she understood they had known
each other in Europe. Naturally, they shared something
of a common background, were friends of long standing.

The terrace had a broad stone balustrade around it,
and Lilli perched on it.

"I shall now tell the story of the origin of chess,"
she began, swinging one foot. "No, don't go, Rudy,"
she interrupted herself to say, as the man made a
move toward rising. "You asked for this lecture, and
even though you know as much about this as I do,
since you asked for it, the least you can do is listen
to it."

She explained that the game was favored among
the upper classes—by royalty, in fact—in the eleventh
century.

"The little town of Strobeck in Germany became
known as 'the chess town' about that time when a count
was imprisoned."

"What was his crime?" asked Rudy, leaning forward
in pretended interest.

"Your guess is as good as mine," retorted Lilli. "Anyway, this count was put into solitary confinement, and being already a chess player—"

"So he didn't learn the game in the chess town?" interrupted Rudy.

"No, he was already an expert. To while away the time waiting for the authorities to decide when and where to hang him, I suppose, he carved a set of chessmen out of wood, chalked a chess board on the stone floor, made his right and left hand partners and let them play against each other. The townspeople, peering through the bars of his cell, grew interested, and he kindly taught them the game. It caught on like—" She paused to pick a dead leaf off the ivy vine that was creeping along the spindles of the balustrade, as it did wherever it was not ruthlessly cut back on this house.

"Wildfire," Rudy finished the sentence for her. He stood up and applauded vociferously.

"But that's not the way I heard it," he said, sitting down again. "I like my version better. It puts the story in the same town, but has an exiled bishop teaching the citizens how to play the game. Later, when he was freed, he came back and founded a school where the children were taught chess along with reading, and so on, and everybody grew up to be chess sharks. . . ."

"Mrs. Wetherby, a gentleman would like to speak

to you on the phone," announced the butler from the doorway.

"Coming," cried Lilli, jumping down from the balustrade. "Shall we say 'continued' and drop your story for the present, Rudy?"

She vanished into the interior of the house.

"Lilli wasn't really interested in my version of the chess tradition, do you think?" Rudy came over and knelt beside Verity's chair. He raised his face to hers, so close that it nearly touched. "But you liked my version better, didn't you?" he asked in an imploring tone.

Verity laughed uncomfortably. Rudy often confused her. "Yes," she murmured now, "I loved your version, but I have to see Aunt Margaret."

"Ah!" said Rudy, rising and offering his arm. "I love you too!"

"I didn't say—" began Verity, but stopped when Rudy laughed.

Chapter 5

After a while Verity began to think that her fears had been unfounded. What had disturbed her, really? Nothing except stealthy noises in the attic above her room, and that might have been due to squirrels or birds that had taken possession of the unused space under the roof. Omar had appeared unexpectedly and seemed to have been following her about. Those warnings Ty had given her seemed to have been based on nothing but his own reactions to various members of the household. Verity decided to ignore all of it—warnings, unexplained sounds, incidents she could not understand.

But her peace of mind was shattered a few nights later when she was again awakened by careful footsteps overhead, the sound of something being moved about in the attic room and, finally, considerable activity in the courtyard below. By parting the ivy with her fingers, she was able to see a station wagon drawn close to a side door. Though she had the window open, she could not put her head out without clipping the ivy with a pair of scissors, so she caught only a glimpse of the car below. She could hear voices. They were low, but the still night carried them to her tower. She could make out only an occasional word, but one of the voices; she was sure, belonged to Jasper Wetherby.

One phrase floated up clearly.

"A big haul," she heard, followed by Jasper's booming laugh. Then: "We'll settle that inside."

There was the sound of a closing door, then silence.

Verity did not hesitate long. She was a half-owner of the business; she was not only within her rights, but owed it to the gallery's clients to investigate any transaction that was even slightly suspicious. She slipped on a robe and slippers and went noiselessly down the stairs to the second floor.

They were probably in the library, she thought. Jasper carried on many business conferences there. Should she go down and, if she saw a light under the door, knock and go in? She could explain that she had heard voices in the courtyard and came down to see if they had visitors. She moved along the corridor, avoiding the front stairway, and reached one of the inconspicuous staircases that seemed to have been built for the express purpose of permitting members of the household to keep from attracting attention as they made their way from one section of the house to another.

Verity remained standing in the dark, against the wall
at the top of the stairs. Was she being foolish? Ty's
words about a fake art plot in Europe came back to her.
Wouldn't it be dangerous if she interrupted a conference of conspirators? She didn't how many were in the
library or, except for Jasper, what kind of characters
they were.

The door to the library opened. Verity flattened herself against the wall, grateful that the light in the library
had been turned off and that the hallway below was dark.
She would not be seen, if no one came up the stairway.

The next afternoon, Verity was recounting the events
of the night to Ty Reynolds. She had called him at the
inn, and when she learned he planned to spend the day
at his typewriter, she asked if she might see him later in
the day. He invited her to have afternoon tea with him in
the garden.

"This is a charming old-fashioned place, run by two
elderly English ladies who count it a favor if anyone asks
for tea at four o'clock. And to suggest that it be served
in the garden—the ladies will love you. They're twins.
Mrs. Hammond is plump and Miss Felicity is thin."

So Verity was leaning back in an old wicker armchair, while one of the old ladies, her cheeks like faded

pink roses, cleared the table, asked if they had enjoyed the crumpets and beamed when Verity was extravagant in her praise of, as she said, something she'd read about in English novels but had never expected to find in this country.

"Not everybody can make them," said the old lady, highly gratified.

"I don't know how to tell you this," Verity said to Ty, when their hostess had gone. "Maybe there's nothing in it, but it seems sort of mysterious to me. Frightening, too."

"Suppose you start at the beginning," suggested Ty.

"No." Verity shook her head, her black hair stirring on her shoulders. "I have to begin with last night, because that's when I really began to be scared. What you said the other day about Jasper Wetherby and the art scandal in Europe—"

She told him of being awakened the night before, by the arrival of a station wagon, footfalls and scraping along the floor of the tower attic, and hearing Jasper's voice from the yard.

"There's a humming bird," said Ty, when she paused.

They both watched the tiny, jewel-colored bird dipping into the flowers on a trumpet vine which clung to a derelict, otherwise bare tree nearby. When the bird darted away, Ty said slowly:

"That wasn't really an attempt to divert you from your story, Vee. I was thinking, and didn't quite know what to say. I don't want to worry you needlessly, and yet—this is the second time you heard these mysterious sounds from the attic, you said?"

"I heard them the very first night I was at Sky Towers."

"Why didn't you tell me about it before?"

"I was afraid you'd think I was imagining things. I didn't hear anyone's voice, to identify it, that first night, either. There seemed to be whisperings above my room— that was all. It might have been squirrels."

"Squirrels can be noisy," agreed Ty. "They can make quite a racket, rolling nuts about. I once lived in a house where I could hear them bowling, or whatever they do with nuts."

"They store them for the winter," interrupted Verity.

"They have fun with them first," said Ty firmly. "But I don't really believe the sounds you heard were made by squirrels, and certainly, unless one of them is a ventriloquist, if you thought you heard Mr. Wetherby's voice, that's just what you did hear.

"However, art dealers undoubtedly get shipments, many of them from Europe, from time to time. They might arrive at Sky Towers at odd times, after being transferred from one of the ports."

"But all the secrecy—"

"Yes, that seems somewhat suspicious," Ty admitted. "But after all, if the shipments arrive late at night, it would seem thoughtless to wake up the whole household. I'm afraid we'll have to assume that Mr. Wetherby is innocent of any fraud in regard to buying and selling art until there seems to be more evidence of guilt. If he chooses to store them in the attic above your room in the tower, he's surely within his rights."

"Haven't I the right to know what's going on?" demanded Verity. "I'm half-owner of the gallery."

"Has anyone given you any information about the way the business of the gallery is conducted?"

"Uncle Timothy's old books were turned over to me, but since I know so little about the art world, they didn't mean much to me," Verity confessed. "Jasper has promised that Lilli will take over my education as an art dealer when I have become more accustomed to my surroundings."

"Well, then, we'll just have to wait, I think. If you get no explanations, or are not invited to look over the current books in, say, two weeks, I think you should ask for a statement on recent events. You say you trust Lilli; you could talk it over with her later on."

The talk turned to Ty's book, and he read the first chapter, which he had modified after seeing the diaries at Sky Towers.

"Why, Ty, you're a genius! Your book will be a best seller. . . ."

"Whoa! The book is only in the chrysalis stage. But it's sweet of you to be so flattering. I wonder—"

"You wonder what?"

"I wonder if I'm doing right to allow you to face unknown dangers at Sky Towers."

"But what can you do? Hire a detective to keep an eye on things? Insist on my moving out of a place that is not only half mine, but one that I've already grown to love? That would be pretty ridiculous, wouldn't it?"

They left it at that. Ty walked with Verity to the garden gate and kissed her—a mere touch of his lips to hers—as they stood facing each other on either side. Verity was happier, somehow, than she had been in days as she started up the drive to Sky Towers. Lilli and her warnings! Ty was not planning to marry her to get control of her fortune; the casualness of his kiss showed that. He was just friendly, taking a friendly interest in her problems at Sky Towers. And because this was so, she was no longer uneasy about the nocturnal activities to which she had been a frightened witness.

"It'll be a young, swinging party," Lilli assured

Verity as they drove to New York, with Jasper and Rudy, to attend an art students' benefit affair on the roof of one of the city's mid-town hotels. They planned to stay overnight, show Rudy Bremer some of the metropolitan sights the next day and perhaps stay a little longer, following their own whims. Rudy, as the only member of the party completely unfamiliar with New York, had announced that he wanted to see "everything," but especially the subway.

They went to the hotel where they were to stay, as soon as they reached the city. It was nearly six o'clock, and the party was to begin around ten, giving them just enough time to rest a bit and dress. They had stopped at a roadhouse on the way down for a snack and meant to save their real appetites for the party itself.

It was well that they did, Lilli observed, when they were confronted with a buffet that included chicken livers with mustard sauce, crab legs and oyster casserole, shrimp and lobster thermidor and even, for the conservative taste, hot macaroni creole. All this, with a variety of salads, little cakes of many kinds, and of course coffee and drinks at the bar.

Those who were not eating were dancing or strolling around the open terrace, which gave a breath-taking view of the city. It was here that Jasper Wetherby and Verity, leaning on the parapet, gazing at the fabulous skyscrapers, got to talking, more by accident than any preconceived intent, about the fake art scandal in Europe. The papers that day had carried headlines about a new development in the investigation, and when Jasper referred to the story, deploring the unsavory publicity, Verity, her recent conversations with Ty Reynolds in mind, unthinkingly remarked that she had heard a great deal about the scandal.

Surprised, Jasper turned to look at her. Many of the windows in the surrounding skyscrapers, brilliantly lighted earlier, had blacked out now, allowing a golden moon to make its radiance felt. It made glistening highlights on Verity's black hair, piled high on her head, and gave additional sparkle to the iridescent beads with which her white gown was almost entirely covered.

"You ought to be painted like that," said Jasper. "It could be called, 'Portrait of a Young Girl in Moonlight.'"

"That's pretty flattering," Verity told him. "But I'd be afraid to sit for a portrait by some of these modern painters. I'm afraid I'd come out looking like something out of a horror film."

"A good description of some of the work of the artists this benefit is meant to help." Jasper laughed and then shook his head. "I think it would be a good idea if our young artists tried to copy twentieth century masters, like Sironi and Morandi and de Chirico. They'd learn more about handling a brush, for instance, than they'd ever discover trying to originate a method before they're ready for it."

"I read in the papers that some European artists are doing just that," said Verity, without stopping to think that her words might betray her suspicions, unformed as they were, about recent transactions at Sky Towers. The next moment she wished with all her heart she could unsay them. "I read about a fake art ring. . . . It doesn't affect us, I suppose. . . ."

Jasper took a step toward her, his face contorted. She hadn't made things better by her added words. "All a scheme to discredit honest art dealers," he told her, biting off his words. Verity noticed that his hands were clenched. "A trumped-up investigation like that could ruin all of us. They're actually charging that some of the paintings signed by the artists themselves—signed, mind you!—are the work of skillful copyists and are being sold as originals."

Now that she had already started something, Verity decided to pursue the subject. "The artist's signature could be imitated, too, couldn't it, if the forger were clever enough to paint a fake picture that would pass the experts?"

Jasper had calmed down a little. "Have you looked

at that de Chirico in our gallery?" he asked. "Of course you have. But have you looked at the back of it, where this artist often signed his name? He has a very distinctive signature. To fake it, the forger would have to trace it by some means, perhaps by photographing a genuine signature and tracing that. But the forgery would be detected by those who know all the forgers' tricks, because no signature is ever exactly like another signature of the same artist. There are always little alterations, so that an exact copy is suspicious in itself."

"I see," said Verity thoughtfully. "This investigation may not be prompted by honest motives, then. I'm afraid I'll never learn the ins and outs of the art business."

"Best to leave matters like these to people who have the training and background for it." Jasper patted her hand where it lay on the parapet; she had turned away to gaze again at the exciting skyline.

Jasper was making her feel like a child. With Lilli on hand to help him run the Sky Towers gallery, he considered any effort on Verity's part to contribute to the business nothing more than interference. But she wanted so much to take a real place in the art world!

Lilli and Rudy joined them just then, declaring that they were missing all the dancing.

"You know I love to dance with you, Jasper," said Lilli. "Come along. I don't see how you've resisted the music so long."

"Well?" said Rudy, when the other two had left, arm in arm. He stood there smiling at Verity. She smiled in return and danced the few feet that separated them. He caught her round the waist and whirled her shoulder-high, picking up speed until one of her silver slippers flew off. Laughing, he set her down, ran to retrieve the shoe and came back, holding it out of her reach.

"Take the other off, too, and you can really go-go," he commanded. Laughing, Verity handed him her other shoe, and he put the pair of them, mostly fragile straps, into his coat pocket.

The dance floor was jammed.

"Poor Jasper!" whispered Rudy as they stood waiting to plunge among the whirling bodies. "He's too old for these gymnastics."

But he didn't sound sympathetic.

Chapter 6

The day of sight-seeing began shortly after ten the next morning. Verity had not realized that the city was so exciting until she began to see it through Rudy Bremer's eyes. Their itinerary took them from Wall Street to the Cloisters at Fort Tryon Park to a tour of the United Nations Headquarters, (where they lunched in the delegates' dining room) to Times Square, where they planned to take the subway to lower Manhattan.

"That ought to be quite a contrast to the medieval monasteries (or parts of them) and the Heroes and Unicorn Tapestries at the Cloisters," said Rudy. His eyes were sparkling with anticipation. Verity wondered at his evident excitement.

"It's nearly five o'clock," she said dubiously, "and the rush hour has already started. We'll be battered, crushed and maybe trampled."

Rudy grinned at her. "That I want to see," he insisted.

Jasper took Verity's arm as they went down the steps, part of a solid phalanx of subway-goers. Rudy and Lilli came behind them single file. Up to now they had managed to avoid getting caught in crowds, having hired a chauffeur-driven limousine for their travels.

Caught up by the horde, all four were carried forward, at a point where a train was loading. As the guard's cries: "Let 'em off!" and "Don't block the doorway!" reverberated over the heads of the crowd and the doors refused to shut because the jammed-in crowd hadn't jammed in quite far enough, he strong-armed the backs of the outer fringe, struggling fiercely to gain the needed inch to get them just clear of the doorway. The guard's determined push did it. The door closed, the train moved slowly, the crowd behind Verity surged forward. Jasper managed to keep hold of her arm, but her hair caught on the button of a man's coat. She wrenched her arm away from Jasper, using both hands to pull her hair loose. She started to speak to Lilli, couldn't see her and at that moment felt herself pushed violently forward. She lost her balance, tottered for a second at the edge of the platform, tried desperately to keep from falling, but, swaying dizzily, fell, with a little cry, into the track pit.

She fell between the rails and lay helpless on the cross-ties, her eyes fixed on what she knew was the lethal third rail.

"Lie still!"

She heard a man's yell, sensed the throbbing of the rails, realized that a train was coming. The man who yelled followed his shout into the pit. She felt herself lifted, thrust toward hands reaching down from the platform. Her rescuer leaped after her, shoving back a couple of onlookers as he landed, and when she looked up at his face, she realized it was not Rudy, as she had expected, but a stranger.

But Rudy was beside her an instant later, gathering her up in his arms, and as the crowd parted momentarily, subdued by the near-tragedy, making his way toward the station wall. Behind her she heard a train roar in, the crowd surging forward again.

Lilli and Jasper were beside her now. Rudy was asking "Are you hurt?" pushing back the hair that had fallen into her eyes.

"I don't think so," Verity managed to gasp, and burst into tears.

"You poor child," said a kindly woman nearby. But Lilli, having worked her way out of the crowd by this time, pushed her aside and put her arm around Verity's shoulders.

"It's shock," she told the men. "We'd better get her back to the hotel, and I'll put her to bed."

But Verity refused to let them make a fuss over her. She dabbed at her eyes with the handkerchief Lilli gave her and announced that they could take her back to the hotel and leave her to take a bath and rest till it was time for them to come back and dress for dinner. Then they could all proceed with their original plan, which included a Broadway show and a night club afterward. She would not let them call a doctor, laughed at the idea of any ill effects that might ensue, told them to go on with their sight-seeing but make it snappy, "because we'll have to cut dinner short as it is," and shooed them out of her room at the hotel.

It was not until they were back at Sky Towers late the following day that Verity had time to try to reconstruct in her mind the events in the subway station. That push that had sent her to the platform's edge had seemed at the time a deliberate act on someone's part, not the generalized pressure of the crowd. But who would have tried to shove her into the track pit? Who, in fact, was trying to kill her?

Alone in her tower room, she called a halt to her thoughts.

Such a thing was unbelievable. Or was it? She remembered Ty's warnings that her life might be in danger if Jasper, for instance, had any inkling that she suspected him of being involved in the fake art ring.

What was it she had said to him the other night at the roof restaurant? Yes—she had told him she'd been reading about European artists copying famous paintings, to pass them off as originals. Jasper had looked so disturbed! And how careful he had been to explain that the investigation abroad was just an attempt to discredit authentic art dealers!

It couldn't have been Jasper who had pushed her off the subway platform. He had been holding onto her arm, and she had pulled away to have both hands free to untangle her hair from that man's coat.

Wasn't it strange, though, that Rudy, who had been on her other side, seemed to have disappeared at the crucial moment? He had not reached out a hand to catch her, and he hadn't jumped down to the tracks after her, either. A stranger did that.

And I never even thanked him! Verity thought ruefully. Then, suddenly, Rudy was right there carrying her away—no use thinking about that now.

No use thinking about any of it, she decided. An accident was an accident, and in a crowd like that—Rudy, she recalled, had never even been in the New York subway before. It was not surprising that he should become separated from her in a mob like that.

I ought to have been able to look out for myself, she thought. "After all, I've lived in New York. I know my way around!"

Should she tell Ty Reynolds about the incident? What was the use? After all, nothing serious had occurred. Probably she wouldn't have given it so much thought if Ty had not been trying to rouse her suspicions against the people at Sky Towers. No use building it up. The best thing for her to do was forget all about the mishap.

Nobody else referred to it, probably because Jasper and Lilli, Rudy and she herself were so busy getting out announcements of a special showing of newly acquired paintings "from an auction of several collections" recently held in Paris. Jasper had a long list of clients, and it was Verity's job to go over his carefully detailed books, which indicated each individual's particular interests. She and Rudy worked together, Verity dictating the clients' names and addresses, with notes about the paintings that might appeal to each.

"Suggest that they make an appointment to see the paintings here," said Verity, as Jasper had told her. "We want to be sure that the special pictures, in each case, are hung in the most advantageous places."

"Mr. Wetherby is very shrewd," observed Rudy. "I

don't believe I'd have thought of that if I'd been running this gallery. Not that that's likely to happen," he added hastily, at Verity's look of surprise. "Even though Jasper is nearly twenty years older than Lilli, he's still what they call in his prime."

"Look here," said Ty, when Verity, her chores with the gallery finished, looked in at the library late in the afternoon. "Here's exciting news. This castle of yours has a secret room—what do you think of that?"

"Where is it?" demanded Verity, perching on the edge of the broad table where Ty had diaries and papers spread about.

"You ask that when it wouldn't be a secret room, would it, if it could be found?"

"I thought maybe they'd left instructions about how to find it," said Verity meekly, swinging her foot. "Doesn't it give even a hint, there in that diary you're reading?"

"Nary a hint, but it has an interesting story, all the same. Did you know you're not far from the 'Great Road' which figured in the Revolutionary War?"

"I didn't even know there was a 'Great Road.' "

"It cut across the Berkshires and was the mountain track along which the Continental fellows dragged the cannon—50 of them—captured at Fort Ticonderoga on Lake Champlain."

"Must have been a tough haul."

"They used ox-carts. They're the cannons the Americans mounted on Dorchester Heights, near Boston, before routing the British out of that city."

"So where does our secret room come in?"

"Don't be impatient. You have to have a little background in order to get the whole picture. A year later, in 1777, when the Americans beat the British in a big battle up this way, they took a lot of Hessian mercenaries prisoner and marched them over the same road. But according to the stuff written here, some of them escaped and found refuge in this castle, which was then in the hands of the British."

"Packed them all in the secret room, I suppose."

Early, Lilli and Rudy were off the next day to Pittsfield, where a large estate, including an art collection, was being sold at auction. Verity was invited to come along at dinner the night before.

"No, thanks, I'd rather explore. Did you see a secret room anywhere about, Lilli?" she asked, "when you were having the place restored."

"I certainly did not," said Lilli. "Where did you ever get such an idea?"

"Oh, in those old papers in the library." Verity glanced at Rudy, who looked eager. "Anybody for exploring—Rudy?"

"He's coming with me. Two experts are better than one, you know, when you're buying paintings at an auction," said Lilli quickly.

It wasn't the first time Lilli had made an excuse to keep Rudy from joining her in a project, Verity thought now. Could Lilli be jealous? No, of course not. She was married to Jasper—and she had known Rudy, she had said, before she married the older man.

"This talk of exploring a place that's half falling down has taken away my appetite. "Aunt Margaret pushed away her plate. "I think I'll go to my room. Unless—" She started to rise but sat down again hastily as a maid came in and set down a loaded tray on a side table.

"What's that for dessert?" she demanded, peering around Jasper's shoulder in order to see.

"Pineapple upside down cake, madam," the maid told her.

"H'm, I just might try a smidgeon of it. Not that Marietta has shown any knack at cake making so far."

The auction was to begin at ten in the morning. A whole day to herself stretched ahead of Verity, as she put on worn denims and a T-shirt. It would have been fun to have Rudy with her, or maybe Ty. Still, it wouldn't hurt to reconnoiter, get the lay of the land, so to speak, and be ready with a general idea of the more intriguing portions of the old house, when she and Rudy —or—Ty—had a chance to explore in good earnest.

She met the butler in a side corridor.

"Which way to the cellars, Soames? I want to do a little exploring."

"Alone? Be careful, Miss Verity. There are parts of the castle not in good repair, you know."

"I know." Verity was impatient. Did everybody take her for a dimwit, who wouldn't notice things such as a hole in a floor or a fallen ceiling?

"This way," said Soames with evident reluctance, and led the way to the kitchen wing and a door that opened on a narrow stairway." The old cellars, I suppose you want. They're never used since Mr. Timothy Wells— your late uncle, miss—or rather Mrs. Timothy had a new utility room built on the first floor."

The stairs were dark. Verity switched on the flashlight she had brought, turned back for a moment to signal, with a circle of finger and thumb, to the worried face of Soames, peering down from the doorway. The cellar door closed above, and she was left alone.

At the foot of the stairs, she turned her light all around the room she stood in. It was empty. The floor was un-paved; probably of hard-packed dirt originally, it was now mostly thick dust.

At least I won't fall through *this* floor. She giggled to herself and set off briskly, her flash trained on the walls around her. Large rough-hewn stones, the interstices filled with smaller stones but without plaster or any other covering, surrounded her. Trickles of water seeped between the stones here and there, glistening under the light. She kept her eyes fixed warily on the walls and tripped, falling headlong over something that cracked ominously beneath her weight. She got to her feet with care.

It was a round wooden cover of some sort. Verity shone her flashlight into the broad space she had made in the old boards when she fell prone on it.

"Water!" She gasped, and drew back. Cautiously moving forward again, she let the light play on the surface of—was it a well? It must be. Mossy stones walled it in. Verity felt suddenly faint. Suppose she had actually fallen in!

For a moment she stood uncertainly, looking back the way she had come, toward the little stairway, half inclined to bolt for it. Why did anyone build this kind of death-trap even in an old cellar?

Then she recalled reading somewhere that in pioneer days, when settlers were besieged by Indians, getting water from an outside well was a problem. Lucky were the people who had a well in their own cellar! Somehow the thought gave her the reassurance needed to go on. Give up her expedition, just because she had found an old well in the cellar? She shook her head at the idea and walked on.

This time she watched the floor rather than the walls. Her feet sank into soft dust, as soft as plush carpets. She turned to look from time to time at the prints she left behind her. She had crossed one empty cellar, and reached another that had cupboards built along the walls. Their doors hung askew on rotten leather hinges, or had fallen off altogether, revealing the remains of shelves.

Storage space for homemade preserves. She smiled to herself, picturing rows of fruit and vegetable-filled jars— did they have glass jars or use earthen-ware ones? As she stood there, she was conscious of the silence around her. She began to walk slowly on.

Strange, she hadn't noticed an echo of her footsteps before. An echo! It couldn't be, not in this dust. She stood still, listening. Not a sound. She took a few steps, very softly. Were those other steps, soft too, practically synchronized with her own?

She changed her pace, walked faster. The other steps, if they were steps, moved faster too. She stopped so abruptly that the footsteps continued for a split-second after her own had ceased, as if they hadn't been able to stop exactly when she stopped so suddenly. Someone was following her—stealthily. Could it be Soames?

Verity gasped. Whoever it was could mean her no good. She was being stalked, perhaps by a killer. Ty had warned her that her death might be welcome to someone —someone who could seize her estate, or someone who meant simply to silence her. She might be suspected of having important information about the fake art ring.

She ran from one cellar into another, aware of footsteps sensed rather than heard. She couldn't keep this up much longer; her chest hurt with trying to breathe. If there were only a way out! A door—

There was a door right under her hand as she touched the wall to steady herself. She had long since dropped the flashlight she had brought and hadn't dared stoop to pick it up. If only this door were not locked! She fumbled at an old latch, lifted it, pulled. The door was not locked.

Carefully Verity opened it just enough to slip through. There was faint light from somewhere, enough for her to see stone footholds, roughly chiseled out of solid rock. She was down them, crossing a space, and ahead of her was a dark opening in the opposite wall.

Crouching in the near-darkness, hearing nothing from her pursuer, she waited a long minute, trying to control her ragged breathing. Perhaps he did not know she had fled through that door. Maybe he hadn't noticed the door himself. If only the door remained shut!

Soundlessly, still crouching, she moved back, past a place where the wall of her retreat jutted out slightly. She waited, but heard nothing. But her glance was drawn back, over her shoulder, as if by a magnet. She hadn't heard the door open, but the beam of a flashlight nevertheless shot through the aperture, illuminating the stone steps for an instant. Whoever held it remained out of sight behind the door. It was just a swift glimmer of light; then it was gone, and there was a faint footfall on the bare stone.

Verity made no further effort to remain soundless. Her pursuer knew where she was; he was stalking her calmly, sure she could not get away. But she'd either make it or die trying! She scuttled on her hands and knees, found after a half-second that the roof above her was giving her room to stand and ran blindly.

Chapter 7

She was in a tunnel. It sloped slowly downward. That, Verity thought grimly, was a break. If it had led upward, she would not have been able to make it, she felt. The rough wall of the tunnel provided an occasional handhold when she stumbled, as she frequently did, for the dirt and stones under her feet gave her only uneasy footing. An occasional rattle of stones behind her told her that her pursuer was still stalking her.

He wasn't trying to overtake her, she realized now. Was he trying to force her well away from the house before he killed her? How far would he let her go?

Distance meant nothing to her now. It seemed endless miles, but she knew it could have been only a few hundred yards—how many yards in a mile? She thought confusedly. She couldn't remember: a hundred, a thousand? How silly to be trying to remember a thing like that, when she was running for her life. Perhaps she was losing her mind. She sobbed beneath her breath.

A new fear struck her. Suppose the tunnel were blocked by a rockfall. How simple it would be for her pursuer to gloat over her helplessness, cornered there, pick up a rock and— Anyway, she'd know then who he was. She knew already who it *couldn't* be. Rudy, of course, had gone to the auction in Pittsfield. Anyway, it wouldn't have been Rudy—why, he liked, maybe really loved her. Ty, of course, was not even to be considered. Omar, could it be Omar? Such a strange man; possibly a homicidal maniac, or a member of some vicious foreign cult, sworn to annihilate as many American women as possible.

Then, to her horror, there was a rockfall! Right ahead of her was a great pile of rocks and earth, as if an avalanche had crashed down on the roof of the tunnel and caved it in. But next minute—oh, beautiful sight!—she saw that in falling the stones and other debris had uprooted a big tree. Lying on its side, the dirt-packed roots and trunk had formed a barrier to some of the falling rocks and left a small open space at one point below the trunk.

Lying prone, she wriggled through, clutching the tree's branches to pull herself to her feet as, drawing in great lungs full of moist air, she looked about her—and saw nothing! She was up against another kind of wall, a wall of fog. It was a thick, wet fog which she could feel against her face.

Since coming to Sky Towers, Verity had become familiar with these mountain fogs. More than once she had watched them rise, apparently out of the ground, and wreathe themselves around the shrubs and bushes in the garden, taking on ghostly shapes before spreading and ascending until they filled the whole atmosphere.

Though she couldn't see a half-dozen feet ahead of her and had no way of finding her bearings, she was rather glad of the fog. If she couldn't see any distance, neither could her pursuer. Heedless of her direction, she walked on quickly, unable to see a tree until she had almost bumped into it.

She found herself in a grove of tangled bushes and low-growing pines. Branches slapped across her face; she knew the pine by its aroma and tried to think where such a grove existed, in relation to Sky Towers. But she had never seen the place before, she was sure.

It was impossible to move quietly. Boughs swished; leaves, sodden as they were, gave out faint sounds at times as her cautious footsteps stirred them. The fog muffled sounds and gave her a false sense of security until a branch snapped sharply, quite near. She was still being followed.

She started to run, but the slap of her moccasins betrayed her location, and she turned in another direction and resumed her careful progress. The impulse to run persisted, and to control it she began to count her steps.

"One, two, three, four. . . ." Was that a stone kicked out of the way of her pursuer? "One, two, three, four," she began, starting the count again. She reached nineteen, discovered that the effort of trying to keep her mind on her counting and at the same time concentrate on possible pursuit was too much for her.

It was getting darker. Was the fog deepening, or was night coming on? Was this a nightmare, from which she would soon wake? Oh, why had she been so reckless as to set out on a trip of exploration alone? If she were killed, it might be days before she was found. She didn't even know if she was beyond the borders of the Sky Towers property.

But she couldn't go any farther without rest.

Must stop. Must stop. She found the words repeated over and over in her weary brain, as she sank to the ground behind a fir tree, its branches growing close to the ground. It was some minutes before her dazed eyes noted the fact that she was in a little pocket formed by three similar trees, completely surrounding her. She just fitted into the enclosure.

Verity drew her legs inside her retreat and sat for a long time. She knew she ought to try to figure out a way to get back to the house, but she was too exhausted to think. Instead, she merely sat staring at the trees, wondering what variety they were. Cedar of some kind, she decided. They grew straight and tall, and in a pillar-like shape. Some day, she thought dreamily, she would like to get a book on trees and identify the species on the mountain that, she realized, belonged partly to her.

I must have run over most of it, she thought suddenly, although I didn't get much of a view. She laughed a little. Some fog!

But memory of her wild struggle through bushes and brambles brought her sharply to attention. It was quite a while since she heard any sound of pursuit—not since she had entered her safety zone, as she called it to herself. Had her pursuer given up the hunt? In spite of her effort to remain alert, her eyes closed. She forced them open again, but soon the lids drooped once more.

I ought to try to get back home, she thought, but it didn't seem to matter just then. She drifted off to sleep.

Something woke her after—it must have been hours later. It was dusk. One of her feet had gone to sleep, too. She moved it, trying to restore the circulation without standing up. It must have been the "pins and needles" in her foot that had awakened her.

No, it had been a sound. She knew that when she heard it repeated. Someone was crashing his way through

trees and bushes. She hadn't escaped after all! Her pursuer had picked up her trail!

She could hear him pushing aside branches now as he
came nearer. The three sentinel trees that surrounded her
would attract his notice, as they had attracted hers. She
cowered down on the ground, then raised her head unbe-
lievingly.

"Verity!" There it was again, louder this time.
Through the trees she caught sight of a glimmer—a flashlight.

"Verity!" That was Ty's voice—or had she begun to
have hallucinations?

"Verity! If you can hear me, answer!"

"Ty!" Her voice was a mere hoarse whisper. She
tried again. "Ty!"

When his face appeared between the branches of two
of "her" trees, she tried to get up, but her sleep-para-
lyzed foot gave gave under her, and she fell back.

"Darling, you're hurt!" Ty was kneeling beside her,
slipping his arm under her shoulders.

"It's my foot!"

"Don't try to stand. Is it broken? I'll carry you!"

At Verity's half-hysterical laugh, he drew back. "Not
broken, she gasped. "My foot's asleep!"

Verity hadn't been far from the house after all. But

it was dark when she and Ty got back, to find everybody, from Jasper, Lilli and Rudy to the butler and the cook, forming a reception committee in the front hall. There were loud words of welcome, and Lilli kissed her, hugging Verity and untangling a small branch that had gotten caught in her hair.

"Too bad we never got that alarm bell fixed," said Jasper. "If she had heard that, Verity could have found her way home all right."

"She should never have gotten lost in the first place," Aunt Margaret, her arm around Verity's waist, said tartly. But the girl noticed that her aunt had tears in her eyes.

"She was lucky to get out of that tunnel alive," put in Ty. "It might have caved in on her."

"I didn't know anything about a tunnel," remarked Lilli. "I wonder why it led out of the cellar."

"I think it must have been an entrance to a mine in the old days. From some of the things I've read in the library here, I know that there were many small iron and lead mines around in pioneer days. Soldiers taken prisoner by the Americans in the Revolution could have used it to escape back to the British lines, if the British sympathizers who owned this castle helped them get away as they were being marched by on the way to an American stockade." Ty stopped and smile deprecatingly. "How

I do run on!" he apologized. "I'm all wound up in the background stuff I've found for my book in this locality."

Lilli glanced at the servants, who were still in the great hall. "How about dinner, Marietta? Miss Verity must be starved, and the rest of us need sustenance, too, after our vigil."

Marietta and the others promptly left, and Omar, who had been standing just inside the door, followed them.

Verity went up to her room to make herself presentable. The others went into the blue drawing room—the smallest of the three—often used for family gatherings. Ty gave them a brief account of Verity's terror-stricken flight, which she had outlined for him on the way back from the woods.

"She was sure someone meant to kill her," he added.

"Omar! It must have been Omar," exclaimed Rudy. "Did you notice how he slunk away just now?"

"Nonsense!" Jasper spoke sharply. "Omar wouldn't hurt a fly, much less Verity. What could possibly be his motive?"

"A sadist. He might just be a sadist," said Lilli.

"I never liked the way his eyes seem to light up when he looked at Verity," put in Aunt Margaret. "I wouldn't want to accuse anyone unjustly, but I think the fellow will bear watching."

"The footsteps I saw in the cellar dust looked too large for Omar," remarked Ty. "Besides, he usually wears those peculiar slippers with the turned-up toes."

"But he has shoes. He wears them when he goes to the village," said Rudy.

"There may be other possibilities," Ty pointed out. "This is a huge place. An escaped lunatic might be hiding out in those empty cellars. Well, we'd all better be on the alert. Meanwhile, if you'll excuse me, I'll go down to the inn and clean up and get into dry clothes. That fog was as wet as a shower bath."

"It's someone who figures you know too much about the fake art ring," Ty suggested the next day, when he and Verity were discussing her experience of twenty-four hours ago. They were sitting on the white iron seat that followed the curve of a semi-circular balustrade of stone. Stone paving made a smooth floor for a semi-circular lookout spot projecting from a broad pathway bordering a cliff at the top of the mountain. Between the garden and this pathway was a wide stretch of lawn, and on the slope of the cliff were flowering shrubs, leading gradually into what looked like a wilderness, but was really an area of trees planted long ago for decorative effect, but now grown into mighty examples of pine and spruce.

"You came out of your tunnel somewhere among those trees, I think," said Ty. "Probably the original tunnel extended for a considerable distance before ending in a mine. There's very likely a connection with an old woods road that led eventually over the mountains and down through the valleys to Canada. But about the man who was following you—he had big feet, by the way, judging from his footprints in the cellar—my own idea is that it might very well be Rudy."

"But it couldn't be!" cried Verity. "Rudy and Lilli were in Pittsfield all day at that art auction, you remember."

"He has an alibi, that's true," returned Ty. "But I can't think of anyone else who would be interested in getting you out of the way."

"It's not Rudy, I'm sure." Verity flushed as she made her spirited defense. "He's not even involved in the ring."

"How can you be sure?"

"He's not the type to belong to anything like a fake art ring. He's a dedicated art lover. He wouldn't lend himself to anything like that. And the idea that he might be trying to kill me—honestly, Ty, I'd laugh if what you're saying weren't so serious."

"I suppose he's been making love to you."

"What if he has?" demanded Verity hotly. "As a

matter of fact, thought, he hasn't. Not love, actually. But he has shown me that he cares. And I think I know why he has held off."

"Why?" Ty looked at her curiously. The lilac color of her eyes had deepened almost to purple; the flush still showed, brightly pink, in her cheeks. She was very lovely.

"Because," Verity said, stammering a little, "he has told me he thinks a marriage between a rich girl and a poor man is unwise. Of course I'm not rich," she added, "but Jasper says the gallery has been showing an increasing profit and if the vogue for modern art continues —have you any notion of the prices some of the art that is popular today is bringing? Hard-edge, color-field and —and I can't remember all the different varieties he mentioned—get fabulous prices. A popular art gallery, and ours is becoming more so every day, is bound to make big money."

"Nice for you," said Ty. Verity detected faint irony in his tone. "And I suppose fake art, forgery of big name art, is even more profitable, since the real artists don't have to be paid."

"I'm surprised you don't suggest that we could go into the business of stolen art and make even more money," said Verity.

"It used to be hard to sell great works of art, since

they are so well known," observed Ty, as if thinking aloud, "but I understand now there may be a market for them behind the iron curtain. You'd have to have the right connections, though." He smiled at Verity. "All this isn't getting us any closer to the problem of who trailed you yesterday, is it?"

"Rudy thinks it was Omar. He said so again this morning." Verity's voice was troubled. "I can't believe that, though. Omar frightens me a little, but he never did anything to make me feel as if he meant me harm. It's just so that he's so different. I don't understand him— and he can hardly speak any English at all. Jasper seems to get along very well with him, though."

"Jasper didn't like what Rudy said about Omar last night, I noticed."

"No, he always say Omar looks after him so well, he wouldn't part with him for the world, or some very serious reason.

"Aunt Margaret is going away for a while tomorrow," said Verity, changing the subject. "She's going to meet some friends in New York, who are giving her a Mediterranean cruise. Rudy is going to drive her down. Of course I'll go along to the city, too, to see that Aunt Margaret gets in touch with her friends. It's nice of Rudy to take her, don't you think? She'll have baggage, and it's such a problem for a woman like her."

"Very thoughtful of Rudy."

"Oh, he said he has business in New York any way. He doesn't have to make a special trip for Aunt Margaret."

"For a minute there I thought it was just a labor of love on his part."

"You don't like Rudy," Verity flared. "You wouldn't have a good word to say for him, no matter what he did. I believe you're jealous of him! I'm sure of it now."

"I'm suspicious of him," retorted Ty. "And while he's off to New York with you tomorrow, I'm going to get one of his shoes and try it for size in those footprints in the cellar."

"Do that," said Verity icily. "And now, if you don't mind, I'm going back to the house."

They walked back to the house without speaking. Ty did not go in, but got his car and sent it down the drive with a furious spurt of gravel by way of goodbye.

Late that evening, when everybody had left for his room, Verity went downstairs to the kitchen for a glass of cold milk from the refrigerator. On the way back she met Rudy in the corridor. He was carrying a broom. Verity stared at it.

"I broke my glass ash tray in my studio," explained Rudy, intercepting her questioning glance. "I thought I'd better sweep it up at once, before one of the maids got a nasty cut."

"Thoughtful of you," said Verity, echoing the word Ty had used about Rudy that afternoon. "Good night."

"Happy dreams," said Rudy.

A thought struck Verity as she went up the stairs to her tower room. Rudy did what he called his own house-work in the studio. *He never let in anyone—even the maid!*

Chapter 8

For the tenth time, as they drove to New York the next day, Aunt Margaret bemoaned the fact that she was going away at a time when she might be needed.

"After what happened to you that day, Verity, I have half a mind to stay and look after you."

"That's nice of you, Aunt Margaret, but after all, what could you do? You were at Sky Towers, you know, and there was nothing you could do to help when I was being pursued all over the place."

"But I did do something. I called Ty when the hours passed and you hadn't returned. He came on the double, I'll say that for him. Not that I have liked the way he seemed to be making a play for you."

"Oh, Aunt Margaret, don't be ridiculous! Ty is only interested in getting historical stuff from our library."

"Whatever his reason for hopping to it when he heard you were missing, he showed a lot of good sense in going about the job of finding you. He asked Soames if he had seen you leave the place, and Soames said no, but showed him the stairs where you went down into the cellars. That's how he got on your trail so quickly."

"I was sure glad to see him, when it was getting dark out there in the woods. I wouldn't be home yet if I'd been trying to find the way by myself." Verity giggled.

"It's no laughing matter," said Aunt Margaret, severely. "That's the trouble with your generation—always ready to make light of really serious situations. All the same, I feel I can go away confident that if you keep close to Lilli and Rudy, they'll look after you. They're right there on the ground, so to speak, and Ty comes and goes. I don't think you'd have gotten into danger if Lilli and Rudy had been home the other day. It was just unfortunate that they had gone to Pittsfield. You should have gone with them . . . but it's over now. Remember what I say and, whatever else you do, keep away from Omar. Though now that everyone practically knows he made the trouble, it's not likely he'll try any tricks again. He knows he's being watched."

"*I* think it's some stranger, an escaped lunatic," said Verity. "Has anyone heard any reports of an escaped inmate of an institution in our neighborhood?"

"Not too recently," said Rudy easily. "But I think Lilli came across a newspaper item like that some time ago. We weren't interested at the time and never bothered to find out what became of him."

"I'll ask Lilli about it when we get back. It's too bad she couldn't come with us today. She loves New York, I know."

"She couldn't possibly leave. A very important client is coming to the gallery today, and Mr. Wetherby was particularly anxious to have her there to discuss a picture the client may buy—at a terrific price. Lilli has all the details on it."

They saw Aunt Margaret settled in the hotel where she was to meet her friends before driving to the dealer's office, where Rudy was to deliver the portfolio of canvases he had brought from Sky Towers.

"Have a stupendous time, and don't win *every* bridge game on the high seas," Verity admonished Aunt Margaret in leaving." You've always been a fiend of a bridge player, and I don't think your game has gone back any, for all your lack of partners at Sky Towers. But try to keep in the good graces of your friends, at least until you're back safe on dry land."

Aunt Margaret laughed and promised.

"And don't worry about me," said Verity finally. "Rudy will take special care of me, won't you, Rudy?"

"Sure will," said Rudy, squeezing Verity's arm as

they stood in the doorway of her aunt's hotel room, smiling goodbye.

They had reached the dealer's address, in the east sixties, before Verity remembered that she had not seen the canvases Rudy was bringing from Sky Towers.

"But I can see them when we hand them over," she said.

"Of course," said Rudy. "But if you don't mind, I'll go in alone and see if Mr.—" he hesitated momentarily over the name—"Mr. Hegerman is ready to receive a visitor. He's eccentric about meeting strangers."

"But I'm part owner of the gallery, Jasper Wetherby's partner!"

"Righto! Naturally Mr.—" again he hesitated over the name—"Hegerman will be glad to see you when I explain who you are. But he's an eccentric. We have to humor him. You do understand, don't you, sweet? When you've been in this business a while longer, you'll realize that everyone connected with it has his idiosyncrasies." Rudy spoke in a half-soothing, half-laughing tone.

Verity nodded uncertainly.

"Won't be a minute," he told her as he got out of the car and went around to lift the portfolio of canvases out of the trunk. She watched him spin through the revolving door. She liked to watch him walk. He has the easy stride of the athlete. Had he ever played professional tennis? she wondered. Or polo? She must ask him about that. He had been so immersed in gallery affairs that he had never taken time for games of any kind since she had been at Sky Towers.

He had said he wouldn't be a minute, and he was back in hardly more time than that.

"The boss wasn't in," he announced. "His secretary was sorry, but he had been called to Washington suddenly and wasn't expected back for a couple of days. I left the paintings with the girl."

"Is that safe?" Verity asked dubiously. "Aren't they very valuable pictures?"

"Yes, but they're safe. Mr. Hegerman left explicit instructions with his secretary about putting them in his special huge safe. I'm sorry you couldn't meet him, though. Better luck next time." Rudy turned to smile at her before starting the car. "Now let's have a good lunch in some smart place and forget business for a while."

It was a very good lunch. Verity was more interested in the other patrons, however, than the food. The handsomely dressed, beautifully groomed women held her attention, and she could have been eating hamburger on a bun instead of an exotic sea food stew, listed as bouillabaisse with saffron on the menu, for all the interest she exhibited in the exquisitely prepared dish.

"Don't look now," she told Rudy, "but that girl three tables away, with the elderly man who looks like a diplomat, has the loveliest red-gold hair I've ever seen."

Rudy managed a surrreptitious glance in the direction indicated. He turned to Verity with a shrug. "Probably a wig. Wouldn't look twice at her myself, while—I suppose you've noticed—I can't take my eyes off you."

"Can't you?" said Verity demurely. "It seemed to me you were charmed by that beef Sukiyaki you've got there."

"I never had it before," Rudy defended himself, grining. "Want to taste it?"

"Golly, no. I've got all the glorified food I can handle right here. I notice the prices weren't shown on the menu. Do they think you'd lose your appetite if you knew what things cost?"

"Jasper Wetherby lent me his credit card," said Rudy lightly. "Paying for all this is his affair."

Before they left the restaurant, they decided to visit an art exhibition that had just opened.

"It's an unusual exhibition," explained Rudy. "Not only is it a hospital benefit exhibition, but it includes more varieties of art styles than you'll usually find in an exhibition or at a gallery. It's to be a quick survey of the whole current field for you, Verity."

"Good," said Verity. "The more I see of modern art, the less I know about it."

"You need a course of study," Rudy told her. "Meanwhile, at this exhibit you'll see everything from pop to representational, including abstract expressionism. How does that sound?"

"It sounds as if you'll have to do a lot of explaining to me. You've no idea of the depth of my ignorance."

"Then that's our program for the afternoon," said Rudy. "We can look in also at the Whitney Museum of American Art in its still new home at Seventy-fifth Street and Madison Avenue. It has been built to provide expanded display areas for American art—painting and sculpture—which has grown to startling proportions in the last few years."

"We don't have representative American art at Sky Towers, do we?" asked Verity wistfully.

"We concentrate on modern European art at present," said Rudy quickly. "Most galleries do have to limit themselves to one type of art, because they want to or because it's practical. Jasper and your late uncle chose to concentrate on such artists as de Chirico, Rossi, Sironi—others of the current European school. Don't let our quick survey of the American field throw you, Verity. Our gallery is doing just fine with its present interests."

Verity enjoyed what she called her "learn-all-about-art" afternoon but admitted that she despaired of ever becoming knowledgeable in the field of art.

"When I listen to you or Lilli, I despair of ever catching up with you two. It's a laugh for me to be co-owner of a gallery. What I don't know about art would fill the Whitney Museum, and I doubt if I'll ever learn."

"You'll learn enough to get by," Rudy consoled her, "especially if you stick with me."

Verity let the phrase go over her head at the time he said it, but later on, when they were back at Sky Towers, she recalled that Rudy's conduct on the way home had given emphatic meaning to his words. He had spoken of marriage, but had not actually asked her to marry him.

They started the homeward drive in the dusk of early evening. A good part of the way was soon behind them, for they took the throughway, mostly non-stop. By the time they were in the mountain area, nearing Sky Towers, they encountered little traffic, late as it was, and on a week day. When Rudy turned off the highway and began to follow a dirt road that climbed a hill, Verity turned to him, surprised.

"Is this a short cut?"

"No, it's the long way home, with a stop-off for intensive observation of the moon."

Verity felt a little electric thrill run through her veins.

Rudy was going to make love to her. She didn't know whether to hope that he would or that he wouldn't.

He stopped the car, and they got out.

"Let's walk a little," Rudy suggested, "at least as far as that boulder over there. It's a natural love-seat, wouldn't you say? Hollowed out on one side to make room for two."

They settled down, and Rudy slipped his arm around her waist. The full moon was misted over—broken bits of cloud kept scudding across it.

"We understand each other, don't we?" murmured Rudy, his lips against her hair.

"Yes, Rudy."

"Then you'll understand that when I tell you to send Ty Reynolds away, to keep him out of the house, I mean it for your own good." He let his lips travel to the side of her face, kissed the lid of the eye nearest him, traveled downward toward her mouth. But she sat up suddenly and turned toward him.

"Send Ty away? Why on earth—?"

"I can't tell you now. But believe me, I know it would be best for you. If you love me—"

"I don't love you," interrupted Verity, bewildered. "That is, I—"

"You're confused, sweetheart. You don't know it, but you do love me. You love me as much as I love you.

Send Ty away. He's trying to break us up."

"There isn't anything to—" began Verity, but Rudy stopped her words with his mouth tight against hers.

"Don't talk. Just feel. You love me. You love me," he murmured.

He drew her into his arms, so that her head was against his shoulder and her face looking up into his. What a strong, exciting face! She put up a finger and touched the firmly modeled chin. He caught the finger in his mouth and tightened his arm about her.

"Say you love me," he commanded after a moment. "I know you do—I can feel the way your heart is beating wildly."

Lying above his own heart, she wondered, without quite realizing that she was wondering, why she could not detect any "wild" heart beat in answer to her own. She did not speak.

"If we were married," said Rudy softly, "we could come to this hilltop, whenever the moon was full, and I'd kiss you like this—and this! Sweetheart, will you send Ty away tomorrow?"

Suddenly Verity felt chilled. To make a request like that, when he had seemed to be thinking only of making love to her! She struggled upright.

"I'll think about it." She had caught a look in Rudy's eyes that struck her as oddly anxious. Why was he so

concerned about Ty? Did he want to get him out of the
way; was he planning to do something he meant to conceal from Ty?

She refused to analyze her suspicions. Rudy was afraid
she would become interested in Ty, of course. He was
merely trying to rid himself of a rival, as any man in
love might do. But the magic of the moment had vanished. And—happy chance!—the moon had disappeared,
and it had begun to rain. Lightly, but still it gave her an
excuse to protest staying any longer. Rudy demurred,
but laughed as he took her arm and started for the car.

"Fraidy cat," he teased. "It's not rain you're afraid
of, either."

It seemed strange, when she got home, that Verity
could not go to Aunt Margaret's room and talk to her
about the day's events, as she had often done. She would
say nothing about the scene on the hill, naturally, but
tell her about the exhibition and the Whitney Museum.
Aunt Margaret would probably have said something de-
rogatory about the eccentricities of modern artists and
architects and sculptors. Her favorite artist was Corot.

"There *were* artists in the nineteenth century," she
always said firmly, when Verity tried to up-date her on
modern trends. "Corot—he painted such restful scenes:
feathery trees, water, usually a cow."

Verity, thinking of Aunt Margaret now, smiled and

wished she could hear her answer to a description of one of the pictures she had seen that afternoon, a geometrical abstraction by John Matt.

In her tower room, Verity got into bed, but she did not go to sleep for a long time. She could hear the rain— it was coming down in earnest now—spattering on the ivy outside her open window. Try as she would to put aside the thought, it kept nagging her awake: why did Rudy want to keep Ty away from Sky Towers?

Chapter 9

Ty had, he told Verity, been very busy while she was in New York. He had arrived the next morning, ostensibly to continue his work on the old diaries. When Verity appeared, ready to copy some of the passages, he was sitting in front of the ancient desk where they were kept. But he had not opened it.

"I have several things to tell you," he told her.

"Fine," said Verity. "I'm in a listening, not a working mood." She settled herself in a big leather armchair.

"I'd rather not talk here. Let's go down to the lake. I don't want to be overheard."

Verity glanced up at him. His face was stern. She rose at once. "Let's," she said. "And why can't we make a picnic out of it? I'll ask Marietta for some sandwiches and we can take the canoe and go far, far away."

As they passed the door to the art gallery, they met Rudy coming out. He eyed the picnic basket Ty was carrying, then gave Verity a significant look.

"A farewell expedition? All the historical research completed?"

The color rose in Verity's face? Before she could speak, Ty answered cheerfully: "Hardly. This is just a picnic break in what promises to be a full summer's work."

"Really?" said Rudy. He stood aside to let them pass.

"Doesn't like me," said Ty under his breath, as they turned into the path that led to the boathouse on the shore of the lake. "I suppose he guesses it's mutual. He'd like me even less if he knew what I found out yesterday."

"How much of this suspense do you think I can stand?" demanded Verity, as they took their careful way down the long flight of stone steps that led to the boathouse at the lake. Years of winter frost and wild storms had uprooted many of the stone slabs, and cracked and broken some of them, so that they gave only insecure footing as the path curved down to the shore.

"I'll give you a hint," said Ty ."What I've found out indicates that Rudy Bremer is a dangerous man."

"I can't believe it," said Verity faintly.

"I'm afraid you'll have to. But wait until we get where we're going, wherever it is, before we go into this."

The canoe was new, one that Rudy had in fact sent to

Sky Towers when he first arrived.

"He's quite a canoeist, I believe," explained Ty.

"He does look as if he could give a good account of himself in all kinds of sports," Verity ventured. "I mean, he has the look of an athlete."

"So you've noticed that." Ty's tone was dry. "And, I gather, so has Lilli."

"What do you mean?"

"Those two seem very friendly to me."

"It would be rather awkward if they weren't, wouldn't it? She's his boss' wife!"

"Skip it. We have more important things to discuss than how friendly Rudy feels toward Lilli."

Ty paddled smoothly across the lake and was following the opposite shore as closely as he dared. "They call this Green Lake," I believe."

"Green Lake is right. It's practically emerald green. When the sun falls on it—do you see?—as it does over there, it sparkles like a real emerald. A kind of jewel dropped down in a depression, a cup, between the mountains." Verity sighed. "It looks so peaceful around here, and yet—"

"It's certainly not as peaceful as it looks at Sky Towers. What do you say we pull in right here? That grassy knoll looks like the perfect picnic spot to me."

"First of all," said Ty, when they were settled, with

the picnic basket swung by its two handles from the
sturdy branch of an old tree, "I have to tell you that
though I managed to sneak one of Rudy's shoes out of
his room yesterday, I had no luck fitting it into those
footprints in the cellar."

"It didn't fit?" Verity's face was bright. "I never
expected it would."

"There weren't any footprints. Someone had swept
them all away."

"Rudy? You thing Rudy—but he was in New York
yesterday with me. Oh!" She stopped suddenly. She remembered having met Rudy with a broom in the corridor that night.

"What's the matter?" Ty saw the startled look on her
face.

"I just remembered something. It has nothing to do
with the footprints, of course. It's just that the other
night I saw Rudy with a broom. He had been sweeping
up the pieces of a broken ash tray."

"Did you see the pieces?"

"No, they were in his studio. Now you're thinking
that Rudy went down and swept away the footprints in
the cellar. That would make him seem to the man who
pursued me, wouldn't it? I shouldn't have mentioned the
broom to you."

"I think you should," said Ty gently. "I'm afraid it

doesn't look good for Rudy, especially with what I got yesterday from a man who lives on a back road that borders on this place. There's an old footpath from the road that comes out on the garden. I happened on it, just by accident, and went down to see where it led. As I reached the road this man, who was going home from the village —he works in a garage there—met me, and we stopped to exchange a few words."

"The villagers like to gossip, Lilli says," observed Verity.

Ty ignored the interruption. "The fellow grinned and said he hadn't ever seen that footpath used so much as he had in the last few days; that it was a tough climb, and he didn't see that it saved much time over the regular drive, because you could walk faster on that.

" 'Who else has been using it?' I asked him," Ty went on. " 'The maids from the village? Not them,' he told me. 'That big young feller from up at the Towers. And to be honest, I only seen him twice, but that was on the same day.

"First time, he got out of the car the old man's wife is always drivin'. That was in the morning. The car drove off—the Missus was drivin'—and Big Boy went up that path you just clumb down. I figured he'd changed his mind about goin' where she was goin'. I was testing a car we'd been repairin' at the garage, and thought nothing of it.

" 'But late in the afternoon—I was comin' home from work, walkin' this time—I see him standin' just about where you are now, as if he had come down that path. Then along comes the car he'd gotten out of in the morning, with the Missus still drivin'. She stopped, he got in, and off they went, toward the driveway of the Towers. I watched. It was quite a ways, but the road bein' straight, I could see the car turn in the gates."

" 'That *was* sort of strange,' I said, 'but there's probably a simple explanation for it.' Do you see what it means, though, Verity?"

"No, I don't."

"It means that Rudy was here at Sky Towers when we thought he was at Pittsfield that day."

"There's no proof. Rudy might have forgotten something and gone back to get it. Lilli might have driven on, to get gas or something, and come back for him."

"But, Vee, that doesn't explain why he was waiting at the bottom of the foot-path when Lilli came back, hours later, as she returned from Pittsfield."

"You're not saying the man actually saw Rudy come down the footpath, are you? Rudy could simply have gotten out of the car again at that place—it might be a good spot to stop a car—and been waiting for Lilli to come back for him from the village where she went to buy something. Unless you actually see something happen, it's just circumstantial evidence, and it's hard to convict a man on that." Verity tried to sound convincing, but her lips were trembling.

"I want to be fair," said Ty, "but the circumstantial evidence in this case seems rather strong, especially when we consider that the cellar footprints were carefully erased."

"I'm still keeping an open mind," retorted Verity stubbornly. "Maybe what you're thinking is true. Maybe Rudy did pretend to go to Pittsfield, and come back secretly to Sky Towers, just to chase me through the cellars. He's a better runner than I am, I should think. He could have caught me before I'd gone very far. But he only *tracked* me. What could possibly have been his motive?"

"He could have wanted to kill you, but wanted to be sure he wouldn't be suspected. He wanted to get you in a place where your—excuse me—remains wouldn't readily be found. Several people must have known you went into the cellars; Soames, for one, and there were probably others. You had to be cornered in a safe place, where the crime wouldn't be discovered very soon."

"I still don't see that he had anything to gain."

"You may be a threat to the fake art ring."

"Ridiculous! Even if Jasper and Lilli and Rudy were mixed up it in any way, *I'm* not involved. I don't know anything about it, except what you've told me. I'm no threat to anyone!"

"And you're the co-owner of the gallery, and Jasper inherits your share if you're rubbed out—I guess that's still the accepted word in gangster circles—and Rudy is employed by Jasper. He's a secretary, but he might perform any number of other tasks, to protect the boss' interests."

"Now I know you're on the wrong trail," laughed Verity. "I know Rudy pretty well, Ty. Your theory may seem plausible, but to someone who knows the man, it's just fantastic."

"Then you think Omar is guilty?"

"No, I don't. I think it's someone like an escaped lunatic, trying to hide out at Sky Towers."

Ty sighed and got up to lift down the picnic basket.

"Let's eat. I've got an idea I'd starve to death before you suspected Rudy, no matter what I said."

When they got back to Sky Towers, late in the afternoon, Soames informed Verity that she was wanted in the library. She found Jasper Wetherby there, with Lilli and Rudy. They all looked serious, and Verity, with a sinking heart, wished Ty had stayed. But he had gone down to the inn.

"Sit down, Verity," said Jasper, as she stood uncertainly near the library table. "Something has come up."

"Everyone who is connected with the art world knows that an investigation has been going on in Europe, of fake art. A large ring, it was believed, has been operating, with clever artists copying mostly Italian art of the first half of this century. Even you knew about it, Verity. You spoke of it when we were at that benefit exhibition in New York."

"I remember. You were annoyed with me because you thought I implied our gallery might be involved. You wanted me to understand that no fake art could possibly be passed off as genuine with you and Lilli to pass on every offering." Verity spoke with assurance.

"I was wrong," said Jasper. "A phony de Chirico was among a recent shipment from abroad. We sold it as genuine."

"But every de Chirico we handled has been signed by the artist," said Rudy. "I am positive of that."

"Even the forgeries," said Jasper, in a chilling tone. "The particular one we are concerned with was signed by the artist himself, but it was a fake, nevertheless. Of course he didn't know it."

"How could that happen?" asked Lilli.

"The man who bought it from us, some weeks ago, became suspicious when a friend of his, an expert in these matters, viewed his 'treasure,' of which he was so proud, and insisted it was a forgery. To settle the matter, the owner had a dealer friend of his take it to Italy and confront the people who executed the sale. To get to the end of the story, the picture has turned out to be a fake."

"But the signature?" Rudy glanced around the circle of faces in bewilderment. "Right on the back of the painting."

"A very clever trick," said Jasper dryly. "A real painting by the artist, done some years ago when he didn't always sign his canvases, was slipped into a frame over a spurious painting. The artist was then asked to sign the painting he neglected to sign years before, and obliged, with his distinctive autograph, never suspecting that he was signing tthe back of a fake painting."

"It's unbelievable!" cried Lilli.

"Not all the pictures faked by the ring were signed in this way," went on Jasper. "In most cases the signatures themselves were forged, as well as the pictures. But in the case of this particular painting we sold, the signature was, as you claimed, Rudy, genuine. But what he signed was a copy of one of his high-priced pictures."

Verity, as she listened to Jasper's explanation, was thinking of that day when she had found Aunt Margaret gleefully recounting what she had seen through the peephole in the wall between her kitchenette and Rudy's studio. What was it he had said? That Rudy wasn't busy painting—he was taking a picture out of a frame. And there was another picture beneath it!

Did that mean—it was not likely. Besides, Aunt Margaret might not have seen what she thought she saw. But Jasper was saying now that he had full confidence in Lilli and Rudy.

"I don't blame either of you. Those fake paintings have been vouched for by some of the finest authorities in Europe.

"I am so worried, though, about our other sales. We've done as astonishing business recently. Suppose we have inadvertently sold other fraudulent paintings as genuine. I am wondering what we can do to correct it." He looked around the circle of listeners.

"Lilli?"

Lilli shook her head. "I'll have to think about it."

"Rudy?"

He said nothing; merely spread his hands in a gesture of perplexity.

"Verity? You're young and new to this situation. Perhaps you have a fresh point of view that will help us."

"I don't know how good my idea is," she said hesitantly. "But I've been thinking, now that the whole ring seems to be about to be exposed, it might be taken as an honest gesture if we wrote those who have bought any questionable paintings, if they'd allow us, in view of the art scandal, to have them re-examined at our expense. If any proved to be forgeries, we could refund the money they paid for them."

"Sensible idea," said Jasper. "We'll kick it around for a couple of days and see what we come up with. Everybody agreeable?"

"Of course," said Lilli quickly. After a minute, Rudy nodded.

Jasper, rising, patted Verity's head in passing. "Got a head on your shoulders," he approved.

Verity sat thinking for a while after the others left. Was Ty right, after all? Was there something wrong at Sky Towers? And—she shivered at the thought—was she in some kind of danger?

It was almost dinner time. She started upstairs to change into a frock, for she was still wearing the denims she had put on for her picnic with Ty. As she rounded the turn on the second floor landing, she met Rudy, who was just closing the gun room door behind him. He whisked something into his trouser pocket as she appeared.

It looked—in the fleeting glance she had of it—like the thugee cord that she had seen on the gun room wall.

Chapter 10

Verity, on her way to Jasper's study the following afternoon, was startled to hear loud voices within. Jasper's voice was raised; he sounded as if he were in a cold fury. Verity could not identify the other voice at first. It was low but menacing, as if its owner were threatening Jasper. As she stood still, not daring to knock, she realized, by the mixture of whatever strange tongue he spoke and his garbled English, that Omar was quarreling with Jasper.

The door flew open, hit the wall behind it with a resounding crash, and Omar strode out. He passed Verity without looking at her and disappeared around the corner of the hallway. At that moment Rudy came out of the library. He was smiling.

"What's the matter with Omar? Do you know?" Verity asked him.

"Jasper fired him. He's enraged. I was watching from

the library door as he went past."

"But why has he been fired? I know Jasper thought a lot of him."

"That was before he gave you such a scare in the cellars."

"But it hasn't been proved that he was even in the cellars that day. I don't think he was."

"Lilli is sure it was Omar. She has never trusted him, and she told Jasper to get rid of him. Jasper didn't want to at first, but Lilli insisted—told him that he was responsible for your safety and maybe her own. Said that the very sight of Omar made her nervous now. And Jasper gave in. He adores Lilli, you know. I think that after the row Omar made just now, he'll be glad he fired him. The man showed his true self in there. He's vicious and resentful. Lilli says he has been positively rude to her more than once. No telling what he'd do if he stayed around here. You're the one who ought to realize that.

"Now, if you'll take my advice and tell Ty to keep away, too, we'll all rest easier around here." Rudy looked at Verity questioningly, but she shook her head.

"No, I can't do that to Ty."

"Then Lilli will speak to Jasper about him, too. As I told you, Jasper will do anything for her."

"Don't say anything to Lilli about this," pleaded Verity. "Give me time to think. I may be able to do it without hurting his feelings."

They left it at that. Verity had no intention of forbidding the place to Ty, however. She was merely trying to gain time to find a solution to the problem.

Ty had left at noon; otherwise she would have asked him to walk with her in the garden. She wanted to tell him what had happened to Omar. If she asked him to intervene in Omar's behalf, he might be able to suggest something that would cushion Omar's harsh dismissal. She went out alone to the garden and walked slowly up and down the winding paths.

Maybe it's all my fault, she thought. If I hadn't insisted on exploring the old cellars, there would have been no incident to make trouble for Omar. And probably Ty would not have annoyed Rudy by spending so much time at Sky Towers, if I had not encouraged him to study the diaries and even helped him with his notes."

In the matter of querying their clients on the subject of the authenticity of paintings recently purchased, as Verity had suggested, Jasper for once overrode Lilli. She offered all kinds of arguments, trying to block the action, but Jasper insisted it was the right thing to do.

"If there have been no other fraudulment pictures," he said, "there's no harm done in asking. If we have sold other fakes, we must make good."

But he put off writing the letters for a few days, to see what was happening in regard to the ring in Europe. Something did happen, too. A request came from the investigators in Italy, explaining that, as the Sky Towers gallery had been a large purchaser of the works of modern Italian artists, they would consider it a favor if they were permitted to send one of their men to examine such recent purchases as they had on hand.

"Rank impertinence!" stormed Lilli." Do they think we are not capable of handling our own affairs?"

"But in one case we already know of, we've proved ourselves careless," Jasper reminded her.

"Just the same, we don't want outsiders prying into our business," said Lilli. "If word of it got out, our fine reputation would be ruined."

Jasper was unmoved, however. Verity, noting his firmness in matters which involved his honesty, had her original faith in him restored. She chided herself for having doubted him a little in the past.

I'll tell him in the morning that I'm sure he's doing the right thing in throwing open the gallery to the investigators, she thought just as she went to sleep that night. I'm co-owner of the gallery, and my opinion ought to carry some weight.

But the next morning, it was too late to tell Jasper anything. He lay dead, strangled, on the floor of the gallery, near an open French window, which was blowing back and forth in the wind, letting in gusts of rain which were making dark wet patches on his pale beige satin dressing gown.

Rudy found him, reporting at his usual nine-thirty at the gallery office. He, Verity and Lilli had breakfasted together. Jasper was absent, but there was nothing unusual about that—he took only coffee in the morning, served by Soames if and when he rang for it.

Verity had followed Rudy into the gallery, looked in, as he did, to find the office empty, and was close behind him when, at Rudy's sharp exclamation as he rounded a screen, she came forward quickly and saw the figure outstretched on the floor, which had been concealed by the screen as they approached it.

Verity screamed. She screamed again and again. Rudy, bending over Jasper's inert body to feel for a pulse, stood up and seized Verity by the shoulders, shaking her savagely.

"Stop it! Pull yourself together!"

Lilli was running into the gallery. "What is it? Why—oh!" She sank to her knees beside Jasper. "His throat! What's that around his throat?"

Rudy drew her to her feet as Soames came to the door, followed by the housekeeper and, a few seconds later, Marietta and the maids, crowding in, looking over each other's shoulders.

"There's been an accident," explained Rudy, his voice grim. "Mr. Wetherby is dead. Will you all go about your usual tasks? I am calling the police."

Verity, silenced by Rudy's rough treatment, stood by the open French door, still banging in the wind. She put out a hand to close it, but let her hand rest on the knob as she stared out at the dripping garden. The pelting rain had whipped whole rows of flowers to the earth; the tall shrubs were bowing their top branches to the storm.

"Shut the window! Don't stand there getting drenched yourself!" rasped Rudy.

Obediently Verity shut and turned the catch of the window. She was in an almost hypnotic state; she would do whatever anyone ordered.

"Somebody's belt—he was strangled by a belt. Whose is it?" Lilli kept muttering. Rudy went to the telephone in the office and called the state police.

"This is Sky Towers. I—we—have just found the owner, Jasper Wetherby, dead. Strangled, I think."

He gave his name, then came out to where Lilli and Verity were still standing where he had left them.

"The police will be right here. Why don't you two go into the library? You can't do anything here."

Lilli burst into loud sobs and turned to go. Verity

went, too, silent, her face set.

Rudy raised his voice after them. "This is Omar's work!" he cried.

Two state policemen arrived with a third man, carrying a doctor's case. An ambulance arrived in short time after. The still form of Jasper, wrapped in a blanket, was carried past the open library door. Verity shuddered violently. It was only when she heard the doors of the ambulance clang shut that she began to cry, as if the sound had somehow released the tears. Lilli, still sobbing, went upstairs.

The police came in to question Verity, but she had nothing to tell them. She had heard no unusual noises during the night. Jasper had been killed between midnight and five that morning, the doctor had estimated. Did he always get up early?

"Sometimes," said Verity. "He told me that the least sound woke him, and when it did, he always went down to the art gallery to see that his pictures were safe."

"Didn't the house have a burglar alarm?" asked one of the policemen.

"Yes," said Rudy, who was standing beside Verity, "but sometimes Mr. Wetherby didn't bother to turn it on. He always said his ears were all the burglar alarm he needed—and much more reliable. He was out of patience with it, ever since it started ringing by accident one night, and nobody could stop it, or sleep either. The repair man didn't arrive till the next afternoon. Everybody went crazy with the noise."

"Humph!" said the policeman.

Ty appeared in the library doorway. Verity had not heard his car, and she stared at him with wet eyes, as if she were seeing an apparition.

"Who are you?" one of the policemen demanded.

Ty explained who he was and why he was at Sky Towers.

"You have a key to this house?"

"No. I generally come in by the kitchen wing, where some of the help see me. Today I came in the front door. It was standing wide open."

"The stretcher bearers must have left it open."

"Stretcher bearers! Is someone hurt?"

"Oh, Ty!" wailed Verity. "Jasper has been murdered!"

"How do you know he was murdered?" asked the policeman sharply. "Couldn't it have been suicide?"

Everybody stood without speaking. Then: "Jasper wouldn't kill himself," said Verity.

When the policemen asked to see Jasper's wife, they were told she had collapsed. The doctor was with her in her suite.

Rudy went upstairs with the policemen. Ty turned to Verity as the sound of their feet on the stairs died away.

"Drowned lilacs," he said, looking into her face.

"What?"

"Your eyes. I'm sorry this happened, Vee. But I have worried about you. It's as if I scented danger in this place. And so, I think, did you."

"Yes," admitted Verity. "But I never thought that Jasper was in danger. I was always scared about myself, though I didn't know what to be scared of."

They sat together in the window seat, looking out at the rain, talking in low tones about the death of Jasper.

"Omar will probably be suspected," said Verity. "He was furious with Jasper when he was fired."

"And the police will get a full account of the quarrel from Rudy."

"I don't believe Omar did it," Verity said.

"Have you any idea who might have wanted Jasper dead? Did he have enemies?"

"I suppose everybody has enemies. But I don't know of any particular person who hated him enough to kill him." Verity, looking out of the window thoughtfully, saw another car, a kind of truck, drive up. "Who do you suppose that is?"

"Probably the technicians. They'll be looking for fingerprints, clues of any kind." Ty shrugged. "We'll all have to come up with alibis, you know," he added.

"You're safe enough, I guess. You can prove you were where you were last night, I suppose. But the rest of us, here in the house! The police will have to take my word for it when I say I went to bed at twelve and didn't leave my room till this morning at nine o'clock when I started down to breakfast. Do you think they'll believe me?" asked Verity.

"I should think they would. You don't look like a girl who could rush a man of Jasper's size and strangle him without protest on his part. What was used to strangle him, by the way? Bare hands?"

"Lilli spoke of a belt around his neck. I didn't look that closely, though. He looked terrible. His face—" Her own face had whitened.

"Never mind. Don't think about it," said Ty. "You've had a fearful shock. Maybe we can go somewhere—just a short drive. . . ."

None of the family or the servants was permitted to leave the estate, however. Ty, after questioning, was allowed to go back to the inn, having been warned to hold himself available for further interrogation.

"If they hadn't sealed off the gallery, I'd try to find

a clue to the murderer," Ty told Verity. " Perhaps I can do a little investigation of my own about the village, however. The people down there are sharp. They may have heard something, seen something that would help. I'll be back later."

Lilli was sleeping. The doctor had put her under sedation and sent for a nurse.

Verity and Rudy had lunch alone. They ate from trays in the morning room.

"I couldn't bear to eat in the dining room—just the two of us," said Verity. The police were busy searching the different rooms. Verity drank her cup of bouillon, and pushed to one side the lamb chop Marietta had sent in. Rudy's appetite did not seem to be impaired.

"It's certain Omar did it," he said. "Is that coffee hot?" He touched the silver coffeepot which the maid had placed beside him. "Ouch! It is. Coffee, Verity?"

She nodded. She wanted an excuse to linger and hear Rudy's reconstruction of the crime, and was prepared to disagree with him as well as she could.

"I told the police about Omar's quarrel with Jasper, his rage at being fired, and before that, his attempt to kill you."

"You shouldn't have said that!" said Verity hotly. "We don't know that it was Omar in the cellar. I still don't think it was."

"You need a lot of convincing," said Rudy. "I only hope your faith in Omar is justified, and that your over-confidence won't prove disastrous."

Ty did not come back. Verity waited restlessly, unable to settle down to anything. The nurse had taken charge of Lilli, and shook her head when Verity asked if she could talk to her. When Ty phoned, it was to report that he had found nothing yet, but was working on something and thought it best to remain in the village.

"There's a man I want to see when he gets home from work," he explained. "He may give me a lead."

Verity, feeling the need to talk to someone, got into conversation with the policeman who was guarding the gallery.

"The belt that strangled Mr. Wetherby—was it his own?" she asked.

"It wasn't a belt. It was a thugee cord," said the policeman. "Friend of mine at the barracks just told me. Do you know what a thugee cord is, miss? Some kind of leather, I think it is, that East Indians used to use for strangling people."

"I know. I've heard of it," said Verity vaguely.

But she wasn't vague about it. Her mind was alerted to the thugee cord on the wall in the gun room. She went up to have a look at it. The space it had occupied on the wall was empty.

Had Omar taken it? Or was that the object Rudy was stuffing into his pocket, as she had thought it might be, that night when she had met him coming out of the gun room? Had Rudy taken it, and not brought it back?

Chapter 11

Jasper's lawyer hired a private detective from Boston, a friend of his. Other police investigators arrived; it seemed to Verity, from then on, that police were everywhere she turned. The doctor made his report; an autopsy proved that Jasper's death was due to strangulation by the thugee cord around his neck. The police set into motion a search for Omar; they seemed to accept Rudy's theory that Omar was guilty. When they dusted for fingerprints, they found everybody's except Omar's—even Verity's. There was a beautiful clear set of hers on the brass knob of the French window that had been swinging wide when Jasper's body was discovered.

"Am I a suspect?" Verity asked the imported detective when she heard about her print on the doorknob.

"No. Rudy explained that he saw your hand on the knob as you closed the door when he told you to. As for the others—it would look suspicious if the family fingerprints and those of Soames and other members of the household staff were not to be found. That would seem to prove that the guilty person's prints had been rubbed out."

"The gallery is dusted every day," remarked Verity. "But Jasper was found early in the morning, before the fingerprints of the day before had been wiped away."

"It seems to me that among all the prints, considering none had been wiped off, there would be some of the strangler's. And they would prove that no member of the household committed the crime."

"No," the detective told her. "It's likely the slayer wore gloves."

A clear pair of footprints had been found on the slab at the foot of the steps leading from the garden to the art gallery, the former patio. They had been protected from the rain by an aluminum awning. They were prints of a pair of odd slippers, shapeless, except that they came to a point at the toes.

"Omar wore slippers most of the time. They turned up at the toes—some kind of oriental slippers, you know."

Ty had been prowling along the shore of Green Lake, following his own line of investigation. When he came up to Sky Towers with a sodden, cheap canvas briefcase under his arm, he looked triumphant.

In a little garden house, where the roof and the vines that covered its sides hid those inside from the house, he opened the case and showed Verity a pair of oriental slippers.

"Omar's! Where did you find them?"

"At the edge of the lake."

"Smart sleuth."

"Not so smart as lucky. I had been thinking that the lake would be a handy place to ditch clues, and I came across a boy—Cleon Mathers, about ten, whom I knew from the village. He was fishing in the lake.

" 'Catch anything?' I asked him.

" 'Yeah—this.' He reached under a bush and pulled out this case. 'Sure thought I had the bag of money they grabbed in that bank robbery. You know the one? But there's nothing in it but a pair of old shoes. I'll throw it back into the lake as soon as I'm done fishing in this spot. I don't want to scare the fish away.'

"I gave him fifty cents for the case, after I saw the 'shoes,' " Ty explained. "They haven't been in the water long. I think they're Omar's."

"But doesn't that prove Omar killed Jasper? They've found footprints of slippers—these probably—leading to the gallery from the garden."

"I think it proves Omar didn't do the crime. I talked

to Omar once about his slippers. He took great care of them—said he couldn't buy replacements in this country. It was raining the morning Jasper was strangled, remember. He'd never come skulking around in the wet garden in those slippers."

"But who—?"

"I don't know who did it, but I think these slippers were used by the guilty man to frame Omar. I'll turn them over to the police, find out if they fit the cast they made of those footprints."

Verity was dubious, but Ty was still elated over his find and, after warning Verity to say nothing about the slippers to Rudy, proposed that they take advantage of his "lucky day" in finding clues, and discover the source of those overhead sounds that had, twice in the short period she had been at Sky Towers, disturbed Verity's rest.

Rudy and Lilli had been called to police headquarters at the county seat.

"We can work on Mrs. Mullins to give us the key to the attic," suggested Ty.

The housekeeper demurred, but when reminded that Verity was a half-owner of Sky Towers and had personal reasons for getting into the tower attic, she handed over the key.

They found the attic filled with paintings, with and without frames. They also found that most of the paintings were signed with such names as Filippo de Pisis, Renato Guttoso, and others which Verity, now somewhat familiar with the paintings handled at Sky Towers, recognized as the names of important twentieth century artists.

"The scrapings and other sounds you heard, those nights when the 'squirrels' were busy, were due to someone moving paintings like these that were either awaiting shipment to dealers around the country or had recently arrived and had to undergo treatment of some kind before being offered for sale. Lilli or Rudy or both are connected with the art forgery ring in Europe, I'm now sure," Ty told Verity.

"But couldn't they be genuine paintings?" asked Verity.

"Some of them may be. But I don't believe the artist Rosai painted three pictures just alike, and all signed with his name. I suspect there's a clever artist at work, who can turn out Rosais to order, and if a dealer's three customers all want the same picture, he hires this artist to produce the picture in triplicate."

"You're right. I wonder if Jasper knew about this. I heard him talking to a stranger the night I heard the last goings-on up here—remember? Do you think that proves he knew this was fake art he was handling?"

"No, I doubt if Jasper examined these pictures. He took Lilli's word that she was dealing with reputable agents in Europe. When any of these pictures were brought down to be hung in the gallery, Rudy took over and prepared them for public appearances in his studio."

"But I can't believe that Lilli is guilty of such faskery, either. Or even Rudy," said Verity.

"I'm afraid they're both guilty. The very fact that Lilli kept you from seeing this collection in the attic is mighty suspicious, isn't it?"

"But there may be an explanation."

Verity clung to this hope, and when Lilli and Rudy got back from police headquarters she brought up the subpect with Lilli. She said nothing about her trip to the attic, however, feeling sure that Mrs. Mullins would say nothing about having given her the key, since she had probably been warned against doing that very thing. She led up to it by remarking that, since Jasper was dead, she supposed there was nothing to be done immediately about the inquiries he meant to make about paintings recently purchased at the gallery.

"Of course not," snapped Lilli. "My husband isn't even buried yet, and you're talking about prying into his affairs."

Verity thought this unfair.

"It's just that I don't like the idea of any charge of forgery hanging over his memory," she protested. "If there should be any fake paintings right now at Sky Towers, we ought to be ready to account for them— alibi ourselves, for instance, by proof that Jasper himself was taking steps to clear the gallery's name.

"Do you think that there might be any such pictures here, anything that one of the investigators from Italy might find?"

This was Verity's loaded question. She hoped that in answering it, Lilli might indicate by words or manner that she was involved in the fake art ring. But Lilli smiled, a sad smile, as she explained that there might indeed be "reproductions" of famous artists' works around the place.

"But they won't be found in the gallery. Perhaps you did not know it, but Jasper was once an instructor in art at a university. He had quite a reputation as a critic, too, and from time to time he still gets paintings by art students, who ask him to criticize their efforts; young students who copy modern Italian artists for practise send their paintings, mostly, because you see our gallery specializes in modern art."

"I didn't know that," Verity admitted. "Jasper always belittled his own knowledge of art. He always claimed that you were the real expert, Lilli."

"That was just a man in love talking." Lilli got out a scrap of a handkerchief and held it to her eyes. "We loved each other so!" Her voice was muffled by sobs, and she ran out of the room.

Sympathetic messages from prominent members of the art world poured in, and Verity and Rudy took over the task of acknowledging them on behalf of Lilli, who was too overwrought to read them, she said. There were so many that Verity was too busy to talk over such new developments as the police divulged, but the authorities continued to be secretive about their findings, so they had very little new information to discuss.

There had been a rigorous examination of Jasper's background, to discover any possible enemy in his past life. Since he was the last member of his family, it was necessary to rely on former associates to reconstruct any kind of story of his earlier days, and nothing was found to provide a clue.

When Ty came up to Sky Towers the day after Jasper's funeral, it was to protest to Verity Omar's arrest. The ex-valet had been taken in custody when he appeared at the funeral, apparently unaware that he was being sought by police.

"Everything points to Omar," Ty said angrily, "but

I should think his going to the funeral would indicate that he never dreamed he was under suspicion."

He hadn't been hiding, Ty went on to say. "The poor fellow admitted he was furious when Jasper discharged him, but he insisted he had not returned to Sky Towers after he was fired. He said, through an interpreter—the police could not follow his garbled answers—that he had not taken any of his belongings with him. He was wearing ordinary shoes when found, and had not even taken his slippers with him when he left.

"He could not understand—'pretended he couldn't understand,' the police say—what had happened to them when they told him no slippers had been found when his room at Sky Towers was searched. When they showed him the slippers Rudy had found at the lake, he admitted they were his, but swore up and down he did not throw them in the lake.

"Do you know what I think, Vee? I think those slippers were meant to be found; that Jasper's murderer used them to throw suspicion on him, and threw them in the lake near enough to the shore to be found, as if Omar himself had tried to dispose of them. If they weren't meant to be found, they could have been destroyed in any one of several different ways."

"Poor Omar," said Verity. "I wish I could help him."

At this highly inopportune time, the investigator for the authorities trying to track down the fake art ring arrived from Italy. He offered condolences to the widow —with Lilli hiding her face in her handkerchief and amazing Verity, who was present, by her replies to his questions.

Jasper bought all the paintings the gallery handled, she said, when asked about the source of the recently bought pictures. But wasn't she a European, active in the buying and selling of art before marrying Jasper?

She was a European, yes, said Lilli, but of no importance in the art world. She was interested in it and sometimes brought young artists she met to the notice of gallery owners, all in the spirit of friendship.

Could the investigator search the house? Since Lilli herself knew so little about art, perhaps there was something she did not recognize as a forgery. . . .

Certainly he could search, said Lilli, if the police had no objections. But the police did have objections. The art inspector would have to wait till they had finished their own search for murder clues. The investigator agreed to wait, took a room at Ty's inn, and he and Ty became friendly enough to discuss Jasper's murder and the art forgery, in general, and in particular, the fake art ring now under investigation.

"He thinks that Jasper's murder is somehow connected

with the investigation of the forgeries," Ty told Verity. They had gone for a walk in the woods beyond the garden.

"That would let Omar out," suggested Verity. "He certainly knows nothing of the activities of the fake ring. Jasper once said he couldn't tell whether a picture was upside down or right side up. In fact, when he was helping in the gallery one day, he did hang a painting upside down."

"I'm no more of a connoisseur than he is," laughed Ty. "Verity darling, do you realize now that Rudy had a special reason for wanting Jasper out of the way?"

"What reason?" asked Verity sharply.

"Jasper was a menace to their safety."

Chapter 12

"We all knew the investigator of fake art was coming here. If Rudy—and Lilli—were involved in some way, they were in danger if poor honest Jasper found out the truth." Ty was very serious.

"But won't they be in trouble anyway, if the investigator finds anything suspicious in the house?" asked Verity.

"They'll gain time, though. Jasper would have acted on any information he received. The investigator will have to go slow, not accuse anybody till he has proof."

They were walking close to the house when they saw, through the open French window of the art gallery, the police inspector and the art investigator talking earnestly together.

"Looks as if they're comparing clues," remarked Ty. "The police might just be wondering if Omar's motive for killing Jasper was the only motive to be discovered around here."

"I wish it were all over," said Verity, sighing. "I'm frightened. Suppose there are more killings?"

"It's smart of you to be on your guard, though I don't like the idea of your being frightened. You've had enough of that, I must say, since coming here.

"I wonder if the police would allow me to move up here for the duration unless things settle down, one way or another? If I could move into your Aunt Margaret's suite, for instance, the servants wouldn't be put to the bother of opening another room. Isn't your housekeeper short-handed, anyway? Didn't you say two of the maids have balked at staying here and have been allowed to remain at their homes in the village?"

Verity nodded. "Yes, they've gone. Mrs. Mullins said she hadn't gotten any work out of them, anyway, since the murder. They refused to go in this room or that, jumped every time a bell rang and burst into tears if someone spoke suddenly."

She considered Ty's suggestion for a moment. Then she said, putting out her hand to touch Ty's sleeve, "I'd feel safe with you here, Ty."

"Then there's nothing to do except fix it up with the police and get together my materials so I can work on my book here. With the police still on guard here, I think you'll be in no danger for a day or so. It's when they leave we'll have to be on the alert, and by then I'll be established up here."

Rudy, having overheard Ty discussing the matter with the police, laughed about it when he mentioned it to Verity.

"Taking advantage of the opportunity to move in on us, is he? Telling him to keep out of the place seems to be having the opposite effect. Was that his answer when you asked him to stay out?"

"I never asked him to stay away, Rudy. I'm a co-owner here and have a right to invite anyone I choose."

"Excuse me for overstepping my authority," sneered Rudy. "I didn't know you were in love with your literary genius."

"Rudy! Please! You know that's not so. You know—"

"That you're in love with me? I used to hope you were—or would be, given time." He looked at her with such heartbreak in his eyes that she was touched.

"Do we have to discuss this now?" she said nervously. "Everything is so disturbed."

"The atmosphere is not romantic, that's what you're trying to say. All right; let's leave it for now. Only, Verity sweetheart, don't believe all that Mr. Ty Reynolds tells you. I trust the fellow less every day."

Lilli heard the news of Ty's proposed move quietly

and offered no objection. "If it makes you happier, or at least more relaxed—I've noticed how badly you feel about Jasper, and how you sympathize with me—it's fine with me. When do you think he'll be here?"

"Oh, after the police go. Whoever killed Jasper— I hope they find him before long—will probably continue to hide out where he is while the police are around. Even insane murderers are very clever in some ways, I've heard."

Lilli gave the sad little half-smile which was all she allowed herself when pleased nowadays.

"Still holding onto your theory, aren't you? But the police have arrested Omar!"

"He's innocent," said Verity firmly.

Verity, asked causually by Police Chief Michael Price when she had last seen the thugee cord before it had been used to strangle Jasper Wetherby, hesitated a moment. Price was a stern-looking officer, tall, heavily built, with a weather-beaten face and pale blue eyes.

"They go through you like a drill," Verity had once remarked to Ty.

Now, under the scrutiny of those eyes, she felt impelled to answer truthfully, even though it meant she was perhaps getting Rudy into difficulties.

"I'm not sure," she said. "That is, I thought I saw

Rudy—Mr. Bremer—slipping it into his pocket as he came out of the gun room. I couldn't stay it actually was the thugee cord that was later—that is—"

"The cord that caused Mr. Wetherby's death," the Chief finished for her, as Verity felt a lump in her throat and could not finish the sentence.

"Did the cord belong to Omar?"

"No," Verity told him. "I believe it was part of Mr. Wetherby's collection of guns and other weapons. He traveled a lot, you see, and he collected guns—and other weapons—as a hobby."

"Did anyone ever explain to you how it was used? Mr. Wetherby—Omar—Mr. Bremer?"

"Rudy—Mr. Bremer—did. I asked him one day how it was handled by an East Indian. I thought it looked rather harmless. Ty Reynolds was with me. We three went up to the gun room, and Rudy showed us how the thugee cord was used. He said it was a trick of the wrist that made it dangerous, and he showed us how it was used to strangle a man."

"Why do you think Mr. Bremer was putting it into his pocket, if that was what he was doing?"

"I have no idea."

"Had Mr. Bremer and Mr. Wetherby quarreled lately?"

"I don't think so. They were friendly. Rudy was

friendly with everyone, except Omar," Verity remembered suddenly.

"What did Mr. Bremer and Omar quarrel about?"

"Oh, it wasn't that they quarreled. Rudy never liked
Omar. Then, when he thought it was Omar who followed
me through the cellars—"

"Was that before or after the thugee cord was missing
from the gun room?"

"That was before. I saw Rudy with the thugee cord
after the scare in the cellars, but before Omar was fired.
He could have put it back, of course; I didn't go to look
again after I first noticed it was missing from the wall."

Verity had previously described her flight through the
cellars. Now, when the officer, after talking to the investigator from Italy, asked if she had any reason to suspect
the Hall of Fame Gallery was handling forged pictures,
she told of Jasper's discovery that one of the pictures
he had sold was forged, and his plans for checking on
other recent sales. The Chief questioned and cross-
questioned her until Verity wasn't sure she wasn't under
suspicion of murdering Jasper, after all.

Lilli began to show signs of impatience with the
police investigation. Both she and Rudy had been questioned at length, going over the same ground that had
been covered with Verity, as they learned by comparing

notes. The police had questioned Rudy about having taken the thugee cord from the gun room. He denied it, and spoke sharply to Verity about telling the officers that she had seen the thugee cord as he put it in his pocket.

"I didn't say I was sure," Verity defended herself. "But I did say the thugee cord was missing from the wall in the gun room when I looked."

"You needn't have said anything about it," said Rudy. "Don't you realize you as good as accused me of taking the cord so I could strangle Jasper?" Verity noticed that his eyes glittered as he spoke, but he gave no other sign of being angry. His voice was softer than usual, in fact.

"I don't think that's true," she said. "You know I wouldn't do anything to hurt you, Rudy."

He regarded her without speaking for a long minute.

"No, I suppose not," he said finally. "And probably it won't matter, once Omar is tried and found guilty. But there's no point in making difficulties for ourselves in the meanwhile, is there? If the police question you again, can't you clam up a little? Spilling everything you know, or think you know, is apt to put all of us in a bad light. First thing you know, you may get into trouble yourself. You're half-owner of this outfit, aren't you? And you don't know when the police will take it into their heads to wonder why you hung around here instead of hiring a competent manager to look after your interests. They know by this time you are no art expert. You're just here to get what you can out of the gallery—one way or another."

Verity was surprised at Rudy's attitude, and poured out her unhappiness and bafflement to Ty when he came up, bringing his typewriter and the notes on his book.

"I have a desk full of material to transfer yet," he explained. "Have the police said when they are pulling out?"

"No, but Lilli is sure they're preparing to close the investigation here tomorrow or the next day. Then you'll move in, and the art inspector from Italy will go to work on the gallery—and Rudy's studio, I suppose, and the tower attic."

"Doesn't Lilli seem worried about what the inspector will find?"

"I don't know whether she's worried or not. She seems to have a lot on her mind. You know the police carried away all the books connected with the gallery. Lilli said a funny thing when they did that. She said she didn't know what they were looking for, but they'd never find it in those books. What do you suppose she meant?"

"Who can guess what either of those two mean? The

only thing I'm sure about right now is that you need pro-
tection, Vee darling."

They were in the library, where he was arranging his
papers in a corner of the big desk. He began to re-
arrange a pile he had just carefully adjusted.

"I want to take care of you always!" he said, turning suddenly. He put his arms around her as she stood
beside him.

At that moment Lilli opened the door.

"I should have knocked, shouldn't I?" She stood
looking at them, a faint smile on her mouth." Anyway,
it's nice to see somebody's happy, not upset by all the
tragedy."

"You don't look too upset yourself," said Ty rudely.
He was furious at Lilli's arrival at that particular
moment. Verity, her color high, tried to smooth things
over.

"You look lovely, Lilli," she said placatingly. "White
becomes you."

"Jasper wouldn't have liked me to go into mourning
black for him, so I'm going to wear white mourning instead."

Lilli's "white mourning" was anything but discon-
solate, Verity was thinking. Lilli's skin-tight sheath of
white brocade looked more like a party dress than
widow's weeds. It was very short, cut low in the neck and

was sleeveless. She was wearing white stockings with—Verity could scarcely believe her eyes—a glint of silver. Her slippers were white.

"I'm not wearing any jewelry," said Lilli virtuously, "except my earrings, of course. Jasper loved to see me wear earrings. 'You wear them as if you were a princess,' he used to say."

The earrings were delicately fashioned platinum, set with the largest sapphires Verity had even seen. The color exactly matched the blue eye shadow, which intensified the blue of Lilli's eyes. For the rest, she was colorless—pale lipstick, gardenia white skin, white nail polish. The effect was striking.

"Are you expecting someone?" asked Verity timidly. She couldn't see Lilli taking all the trouble she had surely taken to present this appearance.

"Jasper's lawyer phoned, asking if he might see me to-day."

"Wasn't he here before?"

"Yes, of course. He came right after it happened. But we didn't discuss business, naturally. I don't think I can talk business this afternoon, either. I feel sick whenever I think of going over poor Jasper's affairs."

"Could I help?" asked Verity. "Anyway, I suppose I ought to listen in. I ought to know how things stand, businesswise. Since I was Jasper's partner—"

"You're my partner now," said Lilli. "There'll be papers to sign, I suppose. But not today—oh, not today! I couldn't endure it! What I'll do, Verity, is arrange with Mr. Dunham—that's the lawyer's name, Charles Dunham—to have a conference with both of us present and settle everything."

"I'd like to meet him today."

"Please, not today, Verity dear. It's too painful for me as it is. You can understand—"

"I'll stay out of his way, then," said Verity. "I do understand how you must feel."

Ty was waiting for her outside the library door.

"I couldn't stay and listen to Lilli feeling sorry for herself," he explained, as he took Verity's arm and propelled her toward the terrace.

"I really do feel sorry for her," Verity told him. "Jasper was a lot older than Lilli, but he was an important man. She probably didn't realize until now how much she relied on his judgment and how much she owed to his position in the social world. He came of a distinguished family, whereas she—"

"Is a nobody," finished Ty. "No one knows her background. In time—and certainly if Jasper had lived she would have become accepted as one of the 'in' people in the art world."

"Do you think Lilli and I can have a good partnership?" Verity went over to sit on the broad stone balustrade. Ty leaned both hands on the wide railing, and stared out at the well-kept lawn.

"I'm not going to answer that until later. It will depend on a lot of things. First of all, I should say, the matter of the fake art ring will have to be settled.

"But I will say this, Verity darling. Whatever happens, I'll look after you, if you'll let me."

"That sounds like a proposal—of a kind."

"It's leading up to one."

"Which will be made?"

"In less public surroundings. Here comes the Police Chief—bent, I judge from his demeanor, on a long and serious confab with you. Therefore I stand not upon the order of my going, but go at once. Shakespeare, slightly revised."

He leaped over the balustrade, waved a hand in farewell and disappeared in the direction of the driveway and his car.

Chapter 13

Ty telephoned that night. He had just received a telegram from his home near Chicago. His father had had a heart attack. Ty was flying out on the first plane he could get, but would be back as soon as possible.

"I hate to leave you, Verity. But if the police are still in the house, I think you'll be safe. Do be careful."

Verity promised, and hoped he would find his father better. Lilli and Rudy were sympathetic and tried to console Verity by saying heart patients often recovered completely these days, with modern methods of treatment.

Verity was surprised to hear considerable movement in the attic as she lay wakeful in bed, feeling somewhat lost with Ty so far away.

I never found out why so many pictures were stored in that little room, she thought. She had not heard the mysterious car drive up, but after a while she did hear it go away. Lilli was evidently doing her best to carry on Jasper's work, she decided, wondering a little why she did not call on Verity for assistance, now that they two were partners.

The Italian art investigator, Fernando Carone, called Verity the next morning to invite her to lunch at the inn in the village. Lilli looked at her oddly, she thought, when Verity told her where she was going. But she told her to have a good time and do what she could to convince the inspector that there were no fraudulent art activities at Sky Towers.

Verity laughed.

"It won't take him long to find out I don't know what I'm talking about when I discuss art."

Carone was charming, and put Verity at ease at once by talking, not about art, but about old houses he had seen.

"I'm going to enjoy investigating Sky Towers," he told her. "I understand it was built nearly two hundred years ago."

"Part of it," said Verity. "It has been expanded and restored and partially rebuilt many times since. I suppose the original house was quite different in many ways from the building today."

She told him about her room in the tower and described the garden.

"The art gallery overlooks the garden. It was a patio, which Mr. Wetherby and my uncle, who was in partnership with him, had roofed over. My uncle was killed in a plane crash some time ago and left his share in Sky Towers to me. I'm trying to learn something about art and about the house itself."

"It's quite suitable that a house like Sky Towers—a castle, really, from what I've heard of it—should be the home of an art gallery," remarked Carone. "Many of the English and European castles, you know, contained famous collections of art, even in the old days."

"Are you familiar with Horace Walpole's book on the pictures of a collection in an old English house, Houghton-Hall, in Norfolk? The book is in a museum, but you may have come across some quotes from it."

Verity shook her head. "I'm a complete ignoramus on the subject of art in any form," she confessed.

"People interested in paintings or the houses of personages of great importance could see them, under certain restrictions. Visitors were supposed to tip the guide, and there was suspicion, in some cases, that the guide was supposed to split with the distinguished owner.

"Walpole issued tickets to those who applied for them, to visit his own house, Strawberry Hill, at Twickenham. But only four were permitted to enter in one day, children were not admitted, and if anybody received a ticket but couldn't use it, he was requested to let Mr. Walpole know, so that someone else could take the tour. He was quite an organizer," said Carone.

"In this country today there is a modern version of this house-viewing custom. In some place whole towns throw open the doors of their show places to visitors for a week or so, for the benefit of some charity, perhaps, or for other community reasons. Visitors pay a fee, of course." Verity smiled. "Most of these houses don't boast great art collections. Probably a few paintings of ancestors represent their art collections!"

"We won't expect to find many classic masterpieces among them," said Carone. "Nor anywhere, for that matter, except in museums. However, there's a big demand for art these days."

He pointed out that there was not even enough latter-day art to satisfy this demand, with authenticated pictures by artists who had in recent years joined the ranks of the classic painters.

"That's one of the reasons, I suppose, for the success of the fake art ring you're investigating," observed Verity.

"No doubt," said Carone. "But this business of fake art, signed with famous names, is not entirely a modern development. Some of our great painters considered pictures done under their supervision were their own and signed them with their own names.

"Rubens was one. Corot was another. Gifted pupils copied their teachers, and in some cases, today, it's a toss-up to decide which is the teacher's and which is the pupil's work."

"Then the artist who copies another, more famous artist's painting and signs the famous man's name to it is not working a new racket," said Verity. "I'm beginning to think I'll never be anything but an innocent bystander in this art game."

"We consider the practise a swindle nowadays," said Carone. "No matter how talented a copyist a painter is, he's a swindler if he forges another artist's name, or manages to get the original artist to sign it by some trick or other."

"They must go to a lot of trouble," said Verity. "There must be a lot of money in it, though, if they can afford to buy a high-priced painting which they want to copy."

"They can sometimes work from photographs," explained Carone. "But it's not just the painting itself that has to be faked. Even the canvas and the paint itself have to be counterfeited. The ring we are investigating in Europe was an elaborate fraud, with technicians and various experts involved in order to 'authenticate' a painting for which it was hoped someone would pay thousands of dollars."

More than ever, Verity felt that her uncle Timothy had let her in for something beyond her ability to handle by leaving her a partnership in the art gallery at Sky Towers. Carone asked her a few questions about the gallery, Jasper Wetherby and Lilli Freer. Some of the questions Verity could answer; most of them she had to shrug aside.

Why, the investigator wanted to know, did she think Jasper was murdered? Did she think Omar had killed him in revenge for losing his job?

"I think he was killed by an insane person or because of something in his past," she said slowly. "But since I know nothing about him except what I've learned since coming here, I can't even guess what it might be. I can't believe that Omar is guilty, somehow, though there does seem to be quite a lot of evidence against him. He was devoted to Jasper, and to have him turn against him the way he did—"

Verity paused.

"Poor Omar was accused of tracking me through the cellars, with the intention of harming—perhaps murdering—me," she went on. "I don't think he was guilty of that, either. I still stick to my theory: it must have been a wandering lunatic. But I have no proof, no clues, even."

They talked awhile longer about the mystifying events at Sky Towers, and Verity said earnestly that she hoped the gallery would be cleared of any involvement in the art scandal, even though one of the Sky Towers paintings had turned out to be a forgery.

"That can be explained, I'm sure. It was an accident, not a deliberate attempt at deception. I have great hopes that you'll be able to give us a clean bill of health, Mr. Carone," she concluded.

Verity walked slowly home and was passing the library on her way to her tower room when she heard the telephone ringing. When she answered it she heard Ty's voice. His tone was disgruntled.

"How nice of you to call me up," said Verity. "How is your father?"

"My father was never better. Somebody was playing a joke on me, sending that telegram."

"Ty! What a despicable thing to do! Would one of your friends be as low as that?"

"If I find out, I'll wring his neck," said Ty grimly. "When will you be back?"

"I already am. At least I'm in New York. I left Chicago as soon as I found out there was nothing the matter with Dad. How are things at Sky Towers?"

"Just the same. The police are still here."

"Good. It won't be long now until I'm there, too."

Lilli had come to the door and heard Verity's side of the conversation.

"You were talking to Ty? How is his father?"

"There's nothing the matter with his father. It was a hoax. Ty is back in New York on his way here."

Lilli commiserated with Verity over Ty's useless trip and told her that the police chief wanted to talk to the three of them—herself, Rudy and Verity—at four o'clock in the library.

"Perhaps he has good news for us. He may have found Jasper's murderer," said Verity.

"Or gotten a confession from Omar," put in Rudy, who had joined them.

Verity turned away from them. "I'll go and fix my hair a little. I must look a sight after that long walk from the village in the wind. I think it's going to rain, the way the wind was blowing."

"Well, well, everybody here?" Chief Price glanced at the three, who were sitting—Verity and Lilli on the cushioned fireside settle, Rudy in an easy chair—waiting for him promptly at four.

He sat down at the head of the library table. "Now, if you'll all come over here—Thank you," as they took chairs alongside the table. "I just wanted to ask you a few questions before we leave."

"The police have finished their investigation here?" asked Rudy.

"For the time being," said the chief. "Mr. Bremer," he looked directly at Rudy, "why did you remove the thugee cord from the wall of the gun room?"

"I?" Rudy returned the chief's stare blandly. "I took it down to show it to Verity here and Mr. Reynolds, who were interested, one day, quite a long time ago. But I put it back at once."

"You showed them how it was used to strangle a person, didn't you?"

"Naturally, they asked me to do that."

"So you are familiar with the use of this East Indian weapon?"

"So, after I showed them, were the members of my audience. Mr. Ty Reynolds was most interested."

"Do you think that either of them would recognize a thugee cord when they next saw it?" The chief looked around at the faces of the others, before returning his gaze to Rudy's face. He said, and his words had the effect of a pounce, "Mr. Bremer, since Miss Welles was one of what you call your audience, don't you think it highly likely that she would recognize the thugee cord if she saw it in your hand, saw you putting it into your pocket, in fact, a short time before Mr. Wetherby was strangled with it?"

"I did not touch the thugee cord after that day when Mr. Reynolds was among those present. I put it back on the wall at that time, and I haven't seen it since." Rudy shot a vindictive glance at Verity.

"But you saw it around Mr. Wetherby's neck when you found him dead in the gallery, didn't you?" purpused the chief.

"Certainly I saw it then. And I knew Omar had put it there!"

"You *knew?*" the chief said, drawling the words a little.

"I guessed," Rudy amended.

"I see." The chief shuffled some notes he had on the table before him. He looked up at Lilli.

"Mrs. Wetherby—" he began.

"I'm known as Lilli Freer—my professional name," said Lilli with a smile.

"Indeed? But you are Mrs. Wetherby, aren't you?"

"Certainly."

"Then we'll use your private legal name, shall we?" the chief went on smoothly. "Mrs. Wetherby, did your husband have many enemies?"

"He had none, that I knew of, until he infuriated Omar by dismissing him."

"He hadn't, for instance, incurred the rage of some buyer who bought, for thousands of dollars, a supposedly genuine painting which turned out to be a forgery?"

"Not to my knowledge." Lilli was suddenly very pale.

"Was your husband in contact with a fake art ring in Europe, having been introduced by you to leading members of this ring when he was on a buying trip to Italy a few months ago?"

Lilli burst into tears.

"Poor Jasper! Now that he can't defend himself, you're accusing him of being involved with counterfeit art dealers!" Lilli dropped her head on her arms, spread out on the table before her, and sobbed heart-brokenly.

"Madam, I have no desire to harass you. I am trying to bring to justice the murderer of your husband," the chief told her.

He began to put his notes together. "I am sorry I have had so little cooperation from Mr. Wetherby's family, with the exception of Miss Welles, who has been most helpful.

"However, I am withdrawing my men from Sky towers, in the belief that the investigation can be pursued more fruitfully elsewhere."

He left the room abruptly without saying goodbye.

There were sounds of departing cars, while the three he had left in the library remained motionless. After a moment Lilli raised her head. Rudy got up. "That's that," he said, and went out, too.

Lilli moved closed to Verity. Her eyes, the girl saw, showed no sign of tears.

"I had such a happy surprise for you, Verity darling," Lilli murmured. "I found that secret room you were talking about, and I meant to take you there right away. But after all this unpleasantness, I suppose you're not in the mood to visit it."

"Of course I am!" cried Verity. "Who knows? It might even give us a clue to the murderer!"

Chapter 14

Lilli took Verity's arm, and together they went up the stairs to the second floor.

"We have to go up to come down," explained Lilli. "There doesn't seem to be any entrance to the secret room on the first floor. We go through the gun room."

"I might have guessed that the tower had something to do with the mystery room," laughed Verity. "Towers have always seemed to have bad reputations in history."

By this time they were in the gun room. The room was paneled in oak, intricately carved, with no visible sign of a door. But Lilli crossed the room and, her hand sliding along the panels, began to count along a line of small arrows carved in the wood.

"It's the only way I can find the spring," she explained. "It's the fifteenth arrow from the carved hand holding a bow, walking clockwise."

At "fifteen," she pressed her whole hand against the

panel, and it swung inward. Verity marveled that Lilli had found it at all.

"Just by accident," Lilli told her.

The open panel revealed a spiral stair that wound downward. Lilli led the way, and they reached a door at the bottom. It was a rusty iron door, and the huge iron key in the lock grated loudly as Lilli turned it.

Inside, there was nothing at all; just a round, empty space with rough stones walls and a stone floor.

"No furniture!" exclaimed Verity. "I thought we'd find an old bed. . . ."

"There are hooks over there on the opposite side," said Lilli. "You can see that there used to be chains holding up a kind of cot."

Verity ran across to inspect the wall. She heard the iron door clang shut behind her and turned. Lilli had gone. The click of the key in the lock from outside shocked her.

"Lilli!" she cried. "What are you doing? Playing a joke on me?"

"It's no joke," Lilli's voice came through the door. It sounded as if she were laughing. "That room you were so anxious to see will be your private mausoleum, honey."

"Lilli, are you out of your mind? Open the door —please! I'm getting frightened."

"You can scream if you want to. No one will hear. There's nobody anywhere near this tower. I'm going, but first I want to let you know how wrong you've been, making up your silly little mind about what was going on here.

"You thought Rudy was in love with you?" Lilli paused for a moment. Verity could hear her scornful laughter.

"What Rudy was doing was keeping you from prying, taking your mind off things like forged art. That's right. Sky Towers has been a haven for forged art ever since Rudy and I came here. We had the right connections in Europe, you see."

"Don't say any more, Lilli! You're making it all up to scare me, aren't you?" Verity's voice broke on a sob.

"Listen, numbskull! Rudy and I compared notes and screamed with laughter, it was so easy to fool you. Rudy and I have been in love since before I married Jasper. Rudy is going to marry me as soon as we get to South America, with all the good paintings.

"Rudy is in the attic now, bringing them to the third floor. I'm going up to help him. He has already cut whatever genuine pictures there are in a gallery out of their frames. We've already managed to transfer a lot of pictures to our agent in New York. Remember the day Rudy drove you and Aunt Margaret into the city and carried a portfolio of paintings into an office? You wanted to see the paintings, but Rudy wouldn't let you. He's very clever, you know."

"You're both clever," said Verity grimly. "But I'll be missed. Someone will find me."

"Wrong again. You'll never be found. Rudy thought of this way of getting rid of you. We knew about this room from the first, while the place was being restored. The workmen showed it to us."

"But you'll be caught, if I die here."

"We won't be caught. Have we been caught by the stupid cops who were looking for Jasper's murderer? Yet Rudy was right under their noses! He planned to use that thugee cord, because it's a simple, clean way to strangle a person and because it would lead the cops to Omar, an East Indian, from the country where thugee was invented.

"Now that you know so much, you might as well know it all. Rudy took Omar's slippers—Omar left Sky Towers in such a hurry after he was fired that he forgot them. Rudy used them to make the footprints outside the gallery, and he threw them in the lake so someone could find them and prove that Omar tried to throw them away."

"Tell me, Lilli, was it Rudy following me through the cellars that day?"

"Of course. He was going to kill you in that tunnel, when you got far enough into the mountain. He didn't know about the cave-in which gave you a chance to get out too soon and escape in the fog.

"Well, I'll be going. Rudy is waiting for me to help him get the pictures into the car that's all set to go. Don't worry about us being short of money. I've got all that Jasper had. I withdrew it from our bank in Pittsfield the day I was supposed to be at an auction. We had a joint account, and I had a forged letter from Jasper, saying we were withdrawing our funds because we were going to settle abroad. The pictures we're taking are worth a fortune in themselves, and we know how to dispose of them.

"Now, if you'll excuse me, I have to go at once. I've a little chore to attend to before I leave Sky Towers. Is there anything else you'd like explained before we leave?"

She waited. Verity made no answer.

"Not talking, eh? Better save your voice for screaming. Start now. I'd like to hear you as I go up the stairs."

Verity, silent on the other side of the door, heard Lilli's laughter, growing fainter as she went up the stairs. She sat down on the stone floor to consider her situation. This couldn't be happening to her. Lilli wouldn't dare! She'd come back and let her out. But the minutes passed. There was no sound from outside. There was also no window in the little cell. The walls showed no chink that would let in air or light. Lilli could have left her the flashlight! It was very dark, and Verity, getting to her feet to examine the walls, was obliged to depend on her hands to search among the rough stones.

Next she turned her attention to the stones in the floor. One of them might conceal a way out. But she could not lift a single stone even a little, though she did manage to get her fingers into one crack. She gave that up, too.

Should she scream? But Lilli had said there was no one in that part of the castle. That, she felt, was probably true. There was no reason for any of the servants to be near the tower, in the late afternoon like this. But there must be something she could do. She started to feel around the walls again.

The air was getting exhausted. It was hard to breathe— she felt as if she were choking. She moved close to the iron door and tried to shake it. But there was no door handle on that side, nothing she could grasp. She felt along the door. It didn't fit very well; it had sagged away from the surrounding frame in the years since the place was built. There was, in fact, a little space along one edge. She couldn't get her fingers in, but she could get more air or—

Was that smoke she smelled?

Verity stood, petrified with fear, for a long moment. The smell grew stronger. She put her ear to the slight open space at the edge. Distinctly she heard the ominous crackling of flames in the distance.

Almost without realizing she was doing it, Verity screamed. Just raw sound, without words, came from her throat. She pounded on the iron door with her fists. Soon it would be hot. There was nothing to burn in the secret room, but smoke and fumes would, she knew, filter in somehow. The air was definitely thick, as if the smoke had already seeped in.

She gave one last, sobbing cry and sank to the floor, unconscious.

When she came to, Verity looked up into a pair of eyes she had never seen before.

"She's coming around," said an equally unfamiliar voice. "You arrived in the nick of time, Mr. Reynolds."

"Dr. Mayer!" someone shouted. "Dr. Mayer!"

The unfamiliar eyes went away, and Ty's were looking down into her own.

"Hi!" said Verity.

"Darling!" Ty knelt beside her and slipped an arm under her shoulders, raising her a little. He bent his head and kissed her gently on the lips before letting her down again.

Verity lay still for a moment, listening to the shouts and the sounds of cars and, far off, a siren. The village below Sky Towers had a volunteer fire department; the firemen were being summoned, she knew.

"I want to see," she said to Ty.

He lifted her promptly in his arms and carried her across the lawn and sat her down on a bench built around a tree. She shivered.

"Here," said Ty, taking off his sweater and putting it around her shoulders. "You're suffering from shock. I'll ask Dr. Mayer to put you in the hospital."

Verity protested so strongly that he dropped the idea.

"I fainted, I guess," she admitted, "but it was as much from fright as from the fumes. I realized the house was on fire and I was trapped. I was sure there'd be no one to save me."

Ty smiled and kissed her again. "Will you be all right for a while if I go see what I can do to help the firemen?" he asked. "There are so few of them, and the place is so big. Promise not to move from this bench." Verity promised and watched him walking swiftly toward the house in the lurid light cast by the fire. Long ribbons of flame shot out of the windows, and from one window a full-length brocaded curtain streamed out, ablaze and fluttering wildly, as if appealing for help.

The fire seemed to be concentrated in the front part

of the house. Heat and flame were scorching the ivy, and some of the vines were already hanging in brown tatters. The firemen, without access to water on the mountain top, concentrated on removing valuables from the house. Ty came by with a load of papers and books from the library—his own notes and the diaries from which he was building a background for his story.

"I just made it with these." He grinned. "But my typewriter is one of the casualties. I had to dive through a sheet of flame to get out—I can't go back."

The rain, which had been threatening all afternoon, came down now, and was greeted with cheers by the fire workers. The roof of the house, along the front, crashed suddenly, sending up a burst of sparks and flying bits of wood from the falling turrets. One of them, almost intact, was hurled into the driveway.

Wistfully Verity stared up at her tower. It hadn't been a happy place, but she had liked it. Now, as the rain came down heavily, the path of the fire was checked. She didn't have to see her tower go up in flames.

Ty came back. "Did everyone get out safely?" Verity asked.

"I'm afraid not. Lilli and Rudy have only just been found, in the old elevator. They are being rushed to the hospital, but Dr. Mayer hasn't much hope. Smoke poisoning. . . ."

"But nobody used the old elevator!" Verity cried.

"It looks as though they were using the elevator to bring down a big load of pictures—the ones we saw in the attic the other day, I suppose. But the elevator, as you say, was not used nowadays, and something went wrong with the mechanism. The cage stuck between the third and second floors, and the door wouldn't open. They had to use acetylene torches to bring them out through the top of the elevator."

"So they didn't get away," murmured Verity.

"Were they trying to leave Sky Towers?" asked Ty sharply. "They weren't supposed to go, were they, while the investigation into Mr. Wetherby's death was still going on?"

"They were fleeing," said Verity. "To South America, Lilli said."

"Lilli told you! What in the world—" Ty stared at her. Then he noticed that her hair was wet, and that water was dripping onto her shoulders from the leaves overhead.

"You're getting drenched!" he cried. "What a dolt I am, Verity! You ought to have been wrapped in warm blankets and put to bed long ago. . . ." He picked her up and started toward his car, which was parked farther down the driveway.

"I can walk," protested Verity. She made a motion

to get down.

"Cut that out," Ty commanded sternly. "You're as light as thistledown, but if you're going to struggle, I'll have to drop you."

Verity subsided meekly and smiled gratefully as Ty deposited her in the car.

"They'll put you up at the inn," Ty assured her as he sent the car down the drive. "They're always asking me about you, ever since that day you made a fuss over their crumpets."

"Maybe they'll make me some again, if I'm staying there," said Verity. "Oh, Ty—" she hid her face against his shoulder, crying brokenly—"it's been terrible! Suppose you hadn't come back from Chicago. Suppose you hadn't found me. . . ." She raised her tear-wet face suddenly. How *did* you find me?" she asked.

"That's a story that can wait," said Ty. They had reached the end of the drive and turned into the village main street. "We'll be in the hotel—to give my little hideaway a dignified name—in another minute. I'll tell my story, and you'll tell yours, which will be a hair-raiser, I'll bet, under more comfortable circumstances for you."

Chapter 15

The inn's landladies couldn't do enough to make Verity comfortable. They gave her a quaint little room, showed her to the nearest bathroom, and after she had had a shower, provided her with an outfit of Miss Felicity, the thin twin. Her own clothes, covered with soot and grime, were consigned to what the English-bred ladies called the dust bin.

In the landladies' private sitting room, Verity was ensconced in a tall-backed armchair, tucked in with extra cushions and would have had a knitted, multi-colored afghan for her knees, except that she protested it was too hot.

Ty smiled at her from the opposite side of the little table. He had roast beef and browned potatoes.

"I see you haven't lost your appetite," observed Verity, as she toyed with the poached egg on toast that had been prepared for her. "I'm not hungry, though," she apologized to Mrs. Hammond, who clucked disapprovingly when Verity shook her head at the homemade chocolate layer cake and said she would settle for a cup of iced tea.

"I'm dying of curiosity," she told Ty, as soon as the table had been cleared. "You must tell me how you ever found me in the secret room, hidden away in the base of that tower, with flames shooting at you from every direction."

"I'll make it short. It wasn't any great sleuthing effort on my part.

"When I reached town, I didn't even wait to phone, but dashed up to Sky Towers to see if you were safe. Well, you weren't, I soon found out.

"Smoke was coming out of the front windows, but I saw no fire yet. Soames, Mrs. Mullins and a girl—a housemaid, I guess—were huddled on the lawn.

"Don't go in," Soames warned me. "The place is on fire, burning in different spots. We ran for our lives as soon as we saw how the fire was running, spreading the floor in little rivers."

"Why, the fire must have been set!" cried Verity. "Kerosene or gasoline must have been poured around!"

"No doubt, but I wasn't concerned with that at the moment. I asked where you were. Soames said Mrs. Freer had told him you went down to the village.

" 'She came back,' Mrs. Mullins added. 'I know she

was with the others, talking to that policeman."

"That was enough for me. I raced for your tower, thinking, darling, you might be overcome with smoke. As I passed the gun room, I noticed the open panel swinging back and forth, and then I heard what sounded like a sob."

"The rest is history. I ducked into the panel, took the staircase as fast as I could—there are drawbacks to trying to leap down a spiral stairs—found the key in the door of your prison, discovered you unconscious and rescued you from your tower, in the true medieval tradition."

"I'm surprised Lilli didn't take the key with her," said Verity, shuddering.

"Lilli locked you in?"

"And liked it," murmured Verity. "Even now I can hardly believe it, Ty. I thought she was a friend. And Rudy—" She stopped to get control of herself.

"Everything you suspected about Rudy is—was—true, Ty. Lilli stood outside the locked door and boasted of the way the two of them had fooled all of us, even the police.

"They were part of the fake art ring in Europe; they were using Jasper's gallery to unload forged pictures; they had stolen all of Jasper's money and were getting ready to flee, as I told you, to South America.

"Lilli told me all this just to gloat over me, since, she

said, I'd never get out of the secret room. I thought then that she meant nobody would find me. I didn't know she and Rudy meant to set the house on fire and cremate me."

"Instead of that they were the victims of their own scheming." Ty's voice was shaken. "They're both dead, Vee. I had a phone call from the hospital while you were dressing."

"They were two such good-looking people—it seems a dreadful waste. Both of them were still young. Ty, Lilli told me something else which you had suspected all along. Rudy, not Omar, strangled poor Jasper. She even told me how he planted a clue with Omar's slippers, to make the police believe Omar was guilty." She yawned suddenly.

"You're worn out," said Ty, "and here I am keeping you talking and living it all over again. I'm a thoughtless idiot. Come on. Up! up!"

He picked her up and carried her in his arms to the stairs.

"You're making a habit of this, aren't you?" said Verity.

"A good habit, though. Don't you like it?"

Verity hid her face against his shoulder. "Oh, yes!" she whispered.

Chief Price dropped in to see them at the inn the next

day. He had a great deal to report.

"It was definitely arson. Sky Towers was set on fire, the fire inspector found. Trails of kerosene had been laid in several of the rooms at the front of the house, where it could be done without being observed by the servants.

"The art gallery was wrecked and most of the pictures destroyed. So were the pictures in the elevator, where Mrs. Wetherby and Mr. Bremer were taking them down to carry them away with them to South America. We checked with the airline—they had reservations."

Omar had been released. He had a substantiated alibi. He had been staying with friends a hundred miles away and, in fact, working as a clerk in their small shop selling "East Indian imports." His time was entirely accounted for.

"I suppose I ought to tell you," began Verity hesitantly, "that Lilli Freer told me—she had locked me in the tower—"

"Mr. Reynolds told me," interrupted the chief.

"You know, then, that she really meant to kill me. She and Rudy had been plotting ever since I came to Sky Towers. At first they wanted just my share of the art gallery; then they were afraid I would inform on them, that I knew about their connection with the fake art ring. But what really decided them, why they chose such a horrible death as locking me in a burning building, seems to have been that they thought I was tipping the police off about Rudy. He did strangle Jasper," she said."

"I know," said the chief. "We were waiting to arrest him until we had enough evidence to stand up in court. But we already had one clue that would have proved his guilt when he came to trial."

"His fingerprints on the thugee cord?" asked Ty.

"Not that. Do you remember what shirt Rudy was wearing at dinner the night before Jasper was killed?"

"I don't," said Ty. "I wasn't there."

"I do," cried Verity. "It was an evening shirt, a very fancy one with tucks edged with very narrow lace down the front. It was an old shirt, Rudy said, not used any more for dress-up affairs, so he was wearing it out around the house."

"His mistake," said the chief dryly. "You know the clothes which Rudy admitted wearing at the time Jasper was strangled were sent to the laboratory to be examined for possible bloodstains or other incriminating evidence."

Rudy laughed about it," Verity remembered. "He said they would find anything to convict him on *his* clothes. And when they were given back to him, he complained that his old shirt was missing."

"The prosecuting attorney had it," explained the chief.

"It was true there was no incriminating evidence *on* Mr. Bremer's clothes anywhere. But there was something *off* Mr. Rudy's shirt. It hasn't been mentioned before, but when the medical examiner took charge of Mr. Wetherby's body, he found, under one fingernail, just a few bits of white thread. Where do you suppose those little threads came from?"

Both Verity and Ty shook their heads, mystified.

"They were torn from one of the narrow strips of lace by Mr. Wetherby in his death struggles as he was being strangled with the thugee cord. He must have clutched at Rudy, trying to reach his hands to tear them loose from the noose he was pulling around his neck, and his fingernails on one hand scratched at the worn lace on Rudy's shirt front, embedding bits of thread under one nail. The torn threads fitted perfectly the place on the lace where they belonged."

"And Rudy never knew that he was not only a suspect, but that the 'dumb cops,' as he called them, had enough evidence to convict him of the murder," said Verity.

"He was smart, but not as smart as he thought," remarked Ty.

"Not quite as smart as the police." Verity smiled at the chief as he got up to leave.

Two letters from Aunt Margaret arrived in that day's mail. One was a picture postcard from the Riviera, where they had made to stop on their Mediterranean cruise. It told Verity how much her aunt was enjoying her trip. The second was an urgent letter from Venice. Margaret had just heard the news of Jasper's murder and ordered Verity to leave Sky Towers at once," before you are strangled, too," and go to a hotel in New York to wait for her "loving and frightened aunt" to return.

Verity and Ty drove up to Sky Towers that afternoon, having gotten permission to enter Verity's tower room and collect her belongings. The tower, and the area around it, had not been touched by the flames, although blackened and impregnated with the smell of fire.

"I've got only summer clothes, fortunately," said Verity, as she stood in her tower room, looking around at the windows, where the ivy was still green on the side away from the rest of the house. "My good coats and suits, such as they are, were stored before I left New York. The things I have here are washable."

"Your Aunt Margaret wasn't so lucky," Ty told her. "The wing where she had her rooms is a shambles."

He helped Verity pack her belongings, and afterward they sat side by side on her wicker settee, and Verity told Ty how much she regretted leaving her garden of nasturtiums—the carpet on her floor.

"Sky Towers will have to be demolished, one of the inspectors told me," he said. "It would cost too much to rebuild, and besides, there'd be no purpose in it. These huge old palaces are no longer practical. They aren't even suitable for conversion into schools or apartments or anything else."

"I'm glad I managed to salvage those old diaries and other papers," said Ty. "And I have had good news about my book. The publisher has accepted it and has sent me a hefty advance, on the strength of a few chapters and an outline."

"Wonderful!" cried Verity. "Oh, Ty, I'm so glad! Something good has come out of Sky Towers after all!"

"I have a plan for all my wealth—all several hundred dollars of it," remarked Ty. His manner was casual.

"Put it in the bank, I hope, and begin to draw interest," replied Verity.

"Bank—pooh! Interest—bah! I have a better plan than that."

Verity turned her lilac eyes on him. What she saw in his face deepened them to the purple which always indicated emotion on her part.

"I'm going to take the money, fly to whatever stopover your Aunt Margaret is luxuriating in and assure her that her niece Verity is fine, just fine."

"Oh!" Verity's voice was small and disappointed. "I'll miss you."

"No, you won't. As Mrs. Tynan Reynolds, you'll be with me, naturally."

Verity laughed. As she had done once before, "Is this a proposal?" she asked.

"It's on the way to becoming one," said Ty gravely. "If I do propose, what do you think you'll say?"

"Whatever you want me to say," laughed Verity.

Ty's arms went around her, and he held her close, looking down into her face.

"Verity Welles, will you marry me?"

"Yes," said Verity.

He pulled her up a little and kissed her, a long, long kiss.

The wind had come up, and the ivy stirred at the window, as she had heard it so many times.

"I think it's whispering about us," murmured Verity when he let her go.

"Yes, and I know what it's saying," said Ty. "It's saying: 'Long life and happiness, lovely Verity, lucky Ty!' "

Corby   c.1

Girl in the tower.